Dogboy:
Den of Thieves

Bill Meeks

MEEKS MIXED MEDIA

Published by Meeks Mixed Media (meeksmixedmedia.com)

Cover illustration by Paul Loudon (paulloudon.com).
Edited by Roxanna Usher

ISBN-10: 1493673831
ISBN-13: 978-1493673834

DEDICATION

To Philadelphia.

CONTENTS

1	Fortune's Fool	1
2	Venture beneath the Skies	13
3	One Face for Another	25
4	Colta City Blues	39
5	The Old Curiosity Shop	53
6	Problems and Bigger Ones	73
7	The Cowboy in the Parking Garage	91
8	Andrus and the Guild of Thieves	109
9	The Guild Strikes!	129
10	Anchored and Sold on a Pillow of Stone	147
11	A Day Out at Dixon Park	163
12	In the Den of Thieves	181
13	Embrace the Underground	195
14	Trouble at Woodrow Wilcox	209
15	The Ghost in the Subway Car	221
16	Escape from the Underground	231
17	The Reunion	243
18	The Thrill of the Forth	255
19	Andrus Revealed	279
20	The Press Conference	293

ACKNOWLEDGMENTS

The biggest thank you goes to my wife for letting me work on this at all hours and listening to me talk about it incessantly.

Thanks to Liam, Liza, and London for being the first test audience and three of the best kids on the planet.

Credit to my collaborators: Roxanna Usher for correction me mistackes, and Paul Loudon (paulloudon.com) for drawing the things I saw in my head.

I'd like to thank Donald J. Sobol, Franklin W. Dixon, Raymond Abrashkin, Gertrude Chandler Warner, Stan Lee, Charles Dickens, Bob Kane, Jay Williams, and all the other writers who influenced the tone of this story.

Finally I'd like to thank my late father, who left behind a black suitcase that was the first building block of this story. Sorry we didn't take better care of it, Bill.

1

Fortune's Fool

Bronson gets in a fight. His family plans a trip.
Duncan packs his trunk. A stranger works on the family car.

Concrete isn't a good material for a bed. It makes great roads, swimming pools, and nuclear power plants, but it doesn't make a good bed. Somebody forgot to tell Bronson Black. He laid flat on his back in the middle of an outdoor basketball court staring up at Arthur Tillman. Arthur was taller than Bronson. He was stronger. Most importantly he was older and meaner.

"So you can't handle a little defense?" asked Arthur. He dribbled a beat up basketball near Bronson's head.

"Don't be a jerk. I'll go home."

"Aw, you hear your mommy calling you for nub-nubs?"

Arthur circled Bronson. He bounced the ball to the right of Bronson's head. *THUMP.* Then to the left. *THUMP.* Bronson jumped up and backed away from the boy.

Bronson stood still. He could feel Arthur moving behind him. *Maybe I should turn around.*

Arthur flicked the back of Bronson's ear. *Okay, guess we're doing this.* Bronson turned around to face Arthur.

Arthur's fist met Bronson's head on the way around. Bronson's legs went limp and he fell down on the concrete for a second time. He didn't want to let on how much it hurt, and he did his best not to cry.

Arthur leaned down and brought his face a few inches from Bronson's. His breath smelled like old potato chips and bubble gum.

"Didn't see that coming?" Arthur asked. "Aw, the

little baby better not cry. Don't cry little baby. Does little baby need his mommy?"

"Is that what you want? Yes, then. Yes, I need my mommy," said Bronson.

Arthur chuckled.

"Sure, I'll bet she has a bottle all warmed up for you." Arthur dribbled his ball back across the court and took a shot.

Bronson was thirteen, practically an adult in kid years, but he was old enough to know that losing a fight meant his life was over at school. He whimpered on the couch while his mother cleaned him up. She took some gauze and poured some alcohol on top. Bronson's father was working at the dining room table. He used a dirty handkerchief to polish a crystal ball.

"I wasn't doing nothing," Bronson said. 'I didn't even look at him. I've got rotten luck."

Bronson's father pulled his reading glasses down and looked Bronson in the eyes.

"Son," he said, "what do I always tell you?"

Bronson knew his father wouldn't let that one

slide. He sat up, sniffled, and parroted back the familiar words.

"We... we make our own luck."

Bronson's father smiled as he came and sat down beside him.

"That's right. We make our own luck, both good and bad."

"But I didn't do anything."

"I know, buddy," his father said, "and it's not your fault. You need to remember that bad luck didn't have anything to do with it. People's decisions caused this. You decided to go there, and he decided to act like a jackass."

"Duncan Oliver Black... watch your language," Bronson's mother said. His dad chuckled.

"Luck is an excuse, and when you start making excuses you stop looking for solutions. We make our own luck, Bron. Never forget it."

"Yes, Dad," Bronson said. He sat up and cleaned the tears off his cheek with his sleeve. "Can I go to my room? I want to forget this whole crummy day."

Duncan put his crystal ball back in the leather trunk where he kept all of his magic gizmos. It was covered in stickers with the names of exotic locales like Jakarta, Amsterdam, and Poughkeepsie. He closed the lid and locked the rusty padlock.

"I've been thinking," he said. "I'm on the road so much... we haven't had a family day out in months."

"A family day out? Like to where?" Bronson asked.

"Well, I guess that's up to you."

"Within reason," Mom said.

"Within reason," Duncan repeated.

Bronson considered the options. They could see a movie. He'd always wanted to visit the Native American reservation and learn how to do a rain dance. Then it hit him. He knew what he wanted to do.

"We can go up to Colta City. I can practice my skating in Dixon Park and we can get some hot dogs at a street cart and then we can visit Uncle Randolph." Bronson had never been to Colta City, and he'd never met his Uncle Randolph. When he thought about his uncle he pictured a guy who had tons of crazy city adventures at coffee shops and delis.

"No," Duncan said, "I don't know if your Uncle Randolph is up for visitors on such short notice. He has a tiny apartment. It isn't set up for thirteen-year-olds. Anyway from what I hear Colta City isn't the safest place these days. They have a lot of problems with street crime up there."

"Aw, Dad," Bronson said, "I'm old enough. Kevin goes up every weekend."

Duncan placed his hand on Bronson's shoulder. Bronson felt a little static shock. Duncan's gaze fixed on the wall like he'd fallen asleep with his eyes open. A few seconds passed then he jerked his hand back.

"Are you okay?" asked Mom.

"I'm... I'm fine. Look, Bron, I'm sure you'll make it up to the city someday soon. I know you will. Tomorrow isn't that day."

Bronson was disappointed, but he could tell it wasn't up for discussion.

"There's the Blue Tip Festival up in Davidson County tomorrow. I guess that would be okay."

"Sounds fine," said Duncan. "We'll head out early. Why don't you help your mom get dinner ready? I've got to pack my trunk for Monday. I'll be upstairs if anybody needs me."

"Hey," Mom said, "you're sure you're okay?"

Duncan picked up his trunk.

"I told you I'm fine. I just need to make sure I'm packed before we head out on our big day."

Duncan dropped the trunk on the floor of the attic. He took out his wallet and produced a small silver key with the initials D.B. carved in it, although the letters were so worn they were almost flush with the key's surface. He unlocked the trunk and took out the dangerous things: fuel for fire eating, throwing knifes, and explosive charges among them.

Duncan took a knife with him to the other end of the attic. He pulled a blanket off a pile of boxes then moved them one by one until he uncovered the floorboards. He jammed his knife between two planks and jiggled it until the left one popped out. There was a large hat box below the floor tied shut with a piece of twine. A word was scrawled on the side of the box: Willowwood.

Duncan cut the twine and put it aside. He

brushed off the dust and took off the lid. There were mementos inside it... echoes of the past. He pulled a square paper package out. He opened the package and made sure everything was there.

He put the package in the trunk, along with all the throwing knives. He locked up the trunk and shoved the key back in his wallet. He felt prepared now and went downstairs to have a good meal with his wife and son.

That night a man sat in a cheap rental car across the street from Bronson's house. He munched on some stale pretzels that he'd opened earlier that day. On the passenger's seat there was a satchel with several compartments. It held a copy of that morning's Colta City Gazette. The headline read "THIEVES TERRORIZE CITY—BUT WHO IS PULLING THEIR STRINGS?"

The windows in Bronson's house went dark. The man grabbed the satchel, dumped the remaining salt from the bag into his mouth, then got out. He closed the door, lifting the handle so the latch wouldn't make much noise. He wasn't used to operating in a nice area, but he knew well enough to stay under the radar of the Neighborhood Watch.

The man skulked down to the end of the block to cross the street, keeping a calm pace at first. As his excitement built he moved faster. He was almost running by the time he reached Bronson's driveway. Sloppy, he thought.

He stopped at the top of the driveway, dropped to his belly, then did an army crawl to the driver's side of the car. He sat up against the door to check the area. The house next door was a concern, but the three-foot brick wall obscured him well enough. He put the satchel under the car then lay down and rolled after it.

He took out a small digital timer with three colored wires hanging off it then used some gaffer's tape to attach the timer to the car. He unscrewed the lid off a small glass jar and pulled out a hunk of what looked to be gray clay. He molded it around the brake line then pressed it together until it was secure.

The man took the red and blue wires and pressed them into the clay then took a little more goop from the jar and placed it over the wires. He fed the blue wire up through the engine, taped it in place, then shut his bag and got out from under the car.

He tried the handle on the car door. It clicked open. Feeling pretty darn lucky he opened the door then felt under the dash for the hood release. He found the handle and gave it a pull—

The trunk popped open.

Add something else to the list, he thought. He felt around until he found a small circular button. He hit the button. The hood clicked open a quarter inch.

He went to the front of the car. A little blue wire poked out from the engine block. He pulled it over to the row of spark plugs. The wire had to be close enough to catch a spark when the engine started but not so close that it would fry out after the car ran a few minutes. Satisfied it was properly positioned he secured it with some gaffer's tape.

He lowered the hood until it rested on the car then pressed down on the hood with his body weight until he heard the click of the latch—

"Gah!"

Slicing pain shot up his spine. He reached behind

his back and felt a fuzzy texture. He grabbed the mystery animal then flung it across the car. It hit the trunk with a *THUD* and let out a screeching "MRRROOWWWW!"

"Stupid filthy cat," the man muttered under his breath. The noise might be a problem, but the trunk was closed. He picked up his satchel and made his way down then across the street. As he made it back to his rental car he heard a familiar voice call out from Bronson's house.

"Who's out there?" Duncan said from his bedroom window.

The man hit the ground. At this point he refused to get caught. He'd already done everything he came to do. There were three separate escape routes but none of them were accessible from his current position. He decided to wait it out.

"Me-ow," said the cat.

"Shoo," Duncan said. "Go away."

The cat darted away to wherever cats disappear to when confronted by strange humans. Duncan sighed and closed the window.

The man counted to fifty before poking his head

up to check the area. The street was as silent as when he got there. He got in the car then played with the radio until he found a soft, soothing female voice to accompany him on his ride back to the train station. He sang along as he drove away.

Doooo doooo doooo, ah ah ah. Doooo doooo dooo, ahhhhhhhh.

2
Venture beneath the Skies

Road trip. Into the woods.
Bronson gets a key. A dog wakes Bronson up for a walk.

Bronson lugged a cooler down the front steps of the house. It only had some sandwiches, sodas, and ice but Bronson wasn't that strong so it took some effort. He put the cooler down behind the car as his parents came out of the front door. Duncan came back to unlock the trunk.

"What's this dent back here?"

"Dent?" Mom said. "What dent? It was fine yesterday."

Duncan pulled a tuft of fur from the foam trunk liner.

"There's our culprit. The stupid cat from last night. It looks like it'll be an easy fix anyway."

"You never know," Mom said, "it could have been the Hough's cat from down the street. I hear she's in a...romantic mood."

Bronson lifted the cooler up and set it in the back. He let out a grunt.

"D'you ever think about lifting, buddy? Maybe that Tillman kid would back off if you bulked up a little."

"I think he's fine just the way he is," Mom said. "He doesn't need to be some tough guy."

"I forgot my comics," Bronson said. "Can I run back inside real quick?"

"If you hurry," Duncan said.

Bronson ran up to his room. He flipped through the uneven stack of comics on his desk. Action Club, Batteryman, Bayou Wraith, and a lot of Spider-Man. He decided on some reprints of Amazing Spider-Man 30-33: The Master Planner Saga. An old villain comes back under a new name and stays in the shadows until he enacts his master plan. It was his favorite comic book story for the moment, although that title was always up for grabs.

He rolled the issues up and bolted back down the stairs. His parents were already in the car. He opened the door, jumped in, then slammed it shut.

"Let's move this thing."

"Hey now," Duncan said, "she may not be a hot rod but I think she'll do just fine for today's venture beneath the skies."

The engine turned over. A shot of electricity traveled up through the spark plug then licked out at the blue wire. The shot traveled down the wire through the engine block until it reached the timer, which clicked on. The display flashed. *29:59... 29:58... 29:57...* The car turned at the end of the block.

Bronson unfastened his seat belt and lay on the floor of the backseat. He kicked his legs in the air. Mom did a crossword in the passenger's seat. She looked out the window at the countryside when her eyes needed some rest. Duncan tapped the steering wheel in time to the song on the radio. The car struggled up a steep hill. They crested the hill and started down the other side.

00:04... 00:03... 00:02...

The timer's display shut off. Electricity jumped through the green and red wires. The clay around the brake line exploded with a small pop.

Duncan noticed the sound. *We'd better check that out,* he thought. He pushed his foot down on the brake pedal. The brakes clicked, then the pedal sunk to the floor. The car picked up speed down the hill. Bronson saw the landscape moving by faster outside the window.

Duncan tried pulling the emergency brake. No luck. He looked down at the bottom of the hill and realized the car was heading for the woods. He figured steering toward the trees was his best chance to stop the car without flipping it. He looked in the rearview mirror. Bronson's legs hung over the top of the seat.

"Bronson," he yelled, "up in your seat this instant."

"Just a second, Dad, almost done."

"I said now! Marsha, get him in his seat and buckle him in...I can't stop this thing."

Mom reached back and grabbed for the scruff of Bronson's neck, but she couldn't quite reach him. She unlatched her seatbelt and leaned over the back of her seat. Duncan grabbed at her blouse and tried to pull her back down in her seat. As he touched her his eyes rolled back into his head. A bright orange flash—

His wife's head flying through the windshield. Blood raining up through black smoke. Pebbles of glass tangling in a web of black hair. The back of her head breaking the windshield. Bronson's body twisting in the air. In the driver's seat he saw...something so horrific he couldn't admit the truth of it to himself. Another flash—

He was back in the car, which surged toward the tree line. He knew he couldn't avoid what was coming...the things from his vision. He turned to his wife, let go of the wheel, and held her cheeks in his hands.

"I love you," he said.

"You...? Will he be okay?" she asked.

"Yes, he'll be—"

The sound of ripping metal. Screaming. Darkness.

Bronson was pretty sure it was night, but he was having trouble being completely sure of anything. All he knew was that he was sore and there was a strong wind blowing through...his head? The trees? The car. He remembered being in the car with his parents. He was reading. That's right. Reading some old comics. He remembered his dad yelling. Something about not stopping something? The car. Dad couldn't stop the car.

Bronson sat up. He bumped his head on something pointy. He reached up to touch the object. The texture seemed familiar. Skin, but cold. He yanked his hand back as his eyes adjusted to the darkness. A shoe... a slip-on... his mother's shoe.

"Mom? Mom, wake up."

The front windshield was shattered. His mom's

upper half was stuck through it. Her blood clung to the pieces of glass, which when combined with the soft moonlight gave them a crimson shimmer.

"She's... gone," said Duncan. His head leaned against the headrest. A soft whine came out whenever he inhaled.

"No, no. She's fine. We need to call an—"

"Son, she's gone. She's been still for hours. I tried—" His body spasmed and he fell against the window. "There's something I need to give you. My wallet. Back right pocket. Hurry."

"No, no, I can go get help." Bronson said. "I can help you, Dad."

"Now, Bronson."

He leaned over the seat. His dad was pinned to it by the steering column. A dark stain seeped through his shirt.

Bronson reached into Duncan's back pocket and pulled out his wallet. He opened it and saw his school picture staring back at him from a thin plastic sleeve. He remembered the day a few months before when they took it.

"There... there is a key behind your picture,"

Duncan said. "Take it out."

Bronson did as he was told.

"Now take my hand. Quickly."

Bronson took his father's hand and squeezed it. He felt a warmth coming from it as it started to glow. An orange aura glittered in the air around their hands and he felt energy crackle through his bones. The aura expanded until he couldn't see anything but orange, then he saw a room. Their attic. Him, in the corner pulling a sheet off some boxes. His dad's magic trunk. Another flash—

The orange light faded and he was back in the car. Blood trickled down Duncan's lips.

"That... what you saw... that is your legacy. Use it. You'll need it soon. There are... people... I—" Duncan's head fell forward. His grip relaxed. Bronson dropped his dad's hand and fell back onto the back seat. He clutched the key tight against his chest.

He decided to play a game with himself. He'd close his eyes for ten seconds and see if he'd wake up. He closed them and opened them and he was still in the car. He tried again and nothing changed. He closed them again and decided to keep them closed as long as he could and maybe... just maybe... it might all fix itself.

Bronson opened his eyes and looked up at the roof of the car. The sun was out. He wasn't in his bed. When he inhaled the hot air burned in his lungs.

Something brushed against his leg. He jumped back against the door of the car. A small dog stared at him expectantly from the other side of the seat. It gave Bronson a sniff then climbed up between his legs.

Bronson didn't want to think about how the dog got into the car. It seemed friendly enough. He pulled on the door handle. It wouldn't budge. He kicked it as hard as he could. Nothing. He kicked it again. The door creaked open a few inches. He pushed it open the rest of the way and climbed out of the car. *Nothing but trees.*

Bronson picked a direction and started walking. When he took a step the dog barked at him. It ran ahead of him then turned around and barked at him again.

Maybe the dog was trying to lead him somewhere? He held out his hand so the dog could sniff him. The dog nudged his shoes with his nose. It ran along a path, looking back every few seconds to make sure Bronson was still following.

They walked along for awhile. Bronson ignored the knot in his knee as he kept pace with the little mutt. They came to a fresh pathway that went up a hill. The dog started up the hill. Bronson followed.

He struggled to keep his footing as the pain in his leg got worse. His foot slipped on a stone. A tear of white pain ripped through his knee. He faltered, and his knee smashed into the stone. He fell face first into a pile of soggy leaves.

The dog nudged Bronson with his cold slimy nose.

Bronson dug his hands into the dewy leaves and pushed himself up onto all fours. He crawled after the dog, afraid to put weight on his knee.

When they reached the top of the hill Bronson got back on his feet and looked around. He saw some gray through the trees a few dozen yards away.

"C'mon, boy. I think we made it."

As they emerged from the trees Bronson saw the

hill where everything went wrong the day before. A chunk of the pavement was missing at the bottom of the hill. The car's bumper laid half on the road and half in the grass.

Bronson stumbled to the edge of the road. The dog sat down beside him. It pawed at his bad leg. Bronson leaned down and scratched the dog behind his ear.

"Thanks, boy," he said.

The sound of an engine came from the east. Bronson looked in the direction of the sound. A red pickup came around the corner. He jumped up and waved his arms.

The car drove a little past them, pulled over, and turned on its hazard lights. Bronson ran over to the car, then realized the dog wasn't with him. He looked back. The dog stood near the trees. He whistled.

"Come on, boy," he said.

The dog didn't budge. They locked eyes. A strong wind blew through the trees and rattled their branches. The dog's eyes sparkled, and he wandered off into the woods.

24

3

One Face for Another

The funeral. The lawyer's office.
Uncle Randolph. A discovery in the attic.
Bronson says goodbye to the Tillman kid.

Bronson sat in a scratched wooden pew in a church he'd never set foot in before. Several women chatted in the pew next to him. His mom used to invite them over for wine and board games a few times a month. One of the ladies, Mrs. More, had been nothing but kind to Bronson in the days since the accident. She'd put him up in her guest room, made him any food he wanted (which wasn't much), and had even purchased the suit he wore to the funeral that day. She sat beside him now as the other adults chatted about how sad the situation was. Everyone agreed what happened to his parents was "just awful." A lot of them referred to him as a "poor boy." A few even called him an orphan.

He'd heard them talking about what would happen to him once things settled down. From what he understood it all depended on the conditions, if any, his parents laid out in their will. Bronson found himself unfazed by any of it. He knew he should care. He missed his folks, but outside that he felt...nothing. *Maybe it hasn't sunk in yet*, he thought, *or maybe spending that night in the car turned me into some sort of sociopath.*

He spun a pink carnation, his mother's favorite, between his thumb and ring finger. He'd picked it on the walk over from Mrs. More's. It hadn't bloomed because of the shadow from the building next door.

The organ started to play. He didn't want to be up in front of everybody during the ceremony so he walked over to the closed caskets at the front of the room.

The preacher, whom he had never met, stood between the two caskets looking appropriately somber. Bronson didn't like him one bit. This guy didn't know his parents. He probably had three of these a week so why would he be sad? Bronson nodded at the preacher and the preacher closed his eyes and nodded back.

Bronson stood in front of his parents' caskets then bowed his head. That's what the adults had done so he figured he'd follow suit. A few of them cried, so Bronson tried to bring some tears to the surface. He figured being at his parent's funeral would be motivation enough, but he didn't have any tears in him. He sniffed a little to keep up appearances.

Bronson laid the carnation on his mother's casket under the spotlight. He wished he could see them one more time for a minute or two. Then he remembered the last time he had seen them and decided against it.

The flower started to open. He loosened his tie. His shoulders shook. He heard a wail off in the distance. It took him a full twenty seconds before he realized the voice was his and ten more seconds to realize he was rocking back and forth on his knees. The preacher placed his hand on Bronson's shoulder. Mrs. More's mumbled something behind him but he couldn't make out what she said. He didn't know where he was or who he was or why he was acting like this.

Bronson stood up straight then straightened his tie. He turned around. Everyone in the building stared at him. Their eyes made him feel small. He ran down the aisle. Mrs. More called after him as he went out the doors in the back. Once he got around the corner he sat on the ground, curled up with his arms over his face, and waited for the whole stupid ceremony to end.

The lawyer's office was mostly empty the next day. Bronson sat up front next to Mrs. More. Wylie Morgan, one of his dad's fellow magicians, stood in the back with his wife. People sat in folding chairs as the lawyer shuffled through documents. A giant clock on the wall struck 10 o'clock. The lawyer stood up.

"We are about to begin."

The lawyer pointed his finger at every person as he counted to make sure everybody was there. He cocked his head to the side and looked down at his sheet.

"We seem to be missing somebody. A Mister..."

The double wooden doors slammed open. A tall man in a trench coat oozed in. Everybody turned to look at him. He seemed to enjoy the attention and did a small curtsy.

"Mr. Randolph Black, bereaved brother of the deceased at your service," he said, "Glad to know each and every one of you fine folks." He took his hat off then held it over his heart. "What a pleasure to know that my brother Duncan touched so many people in his too-short life."

He dashed over to Bronson and knelt down beside him.

"You must be Bronson. I wish I could say I'd heard a lot about you, but sadly your father thought it best to not tell me much. Thrilled to know you, my boy. You have a hard life ahead of you with no parents and all. I hope they saw fit to leave you something anyway."

Randolph wasn't anything like Bronson imagined. He always pictured him as a younger, cooler version of his dad. The man before him was a scoundrel at least. He seemed like the type of person you'd find in a dark alleyway, but he carried himself like a nobleman.

"Mr. Black," the lawyer said, "if you could find a seat we are about to begin."

"Oh yes, sir. Of course, sir. Pardon the interruption, sir. I'll sit back here, sir." He went to the back row of folding chairs, plopped down, put his feet up, folded his arms, and stared up at the ceiling.

"Yes," the lawyer said, "we'll begin then. Now, we are all here to hear the final instructions for the estate of Mr. and Mrs. Duncan Black, survived by their son Bronson. Now, there's not a lot to tell. Mr. Black was a traveling magician. He didn't have much in the way of hard assets. Some savings, no pension, and he didn't own any property."

"You're kidding," chimed in Randolph from the back.

"Sir, I'll ask that you keep quiet so that we can proceed in due course. Now, Mr. Black's $15,000 in savings will be split in half. Half will pay for a storage unit for the family's belongings until his son turns 21, and half will go into a certificate of deposit until his 23rd birthday, after which it will be released to him."

Randolph put on his hat then stomped back toward the door.

"Mr. Black, please sit down. We will get to you in a moment."

Annoyed, Randolph went back to his seat. He pulled a small knife from one pocket and an apple from another. He cut off a hunk and sucked it into his mouth. Juice spat from his lips and hit Mrs. More on the back of the neck.

"Now then," the lawyer said, "the car, as we all know, was a complete loss. They did have a small insurance policy. Unfortunately the accident was deemed an "act of God." The policy only covers the fees for the tow and ambulance. Now, to Mr. Wylie Morgan is left all of Mr. Duncan's intellectual property, i.e., his magic tricks, patents, etc., with which Mr. Morgan is free to perform or sell as he wishes, although the deceased did note that he would prefer they not be sold. To Mr. Randolph Black is left…"

"Well it ain't like there's much left, is it?" Randolph said with a mouth full of mauled apple chunks.

"To Mr. Randolph Black," continued the lawyer, "or to be more specific 'the closest related family member,' the deceased leave custody of their beloved son Bronson."

Randolph spit the apple cud he'd been chewing into a potted plant beside him. He pushed his sunglasses down to the tip of his nose. "You're serious?" he asked.

"I assure you, Mr. Black. I am never not serious."

"Gee," Randolph said. He pointed the knife at Bronson then clicked it closed, "Thanks, brother."

Bronson was in his room packing up his stuff for his big move to Colta City. He assumed it would be his last night at home. On one hand he couldn't believe he was going; on the other hand he couldn't believe who he was going with. Randolph stood in the doorway watching his every move. Any time he would open a drawer Randolph would peer over his should to inspect the contents.

"Your parents didn't give you much, did they,

Bronson?" he asked.

"They always gave me what I needed."

"Clothes, shoes, a few baubles here and there. I don't see anything of value."

Bronson felt more uneasy about his uncle by the moment. "My dad never talked much about you, Uncle Randolph. Why not?"

Randolph seized one of Bronson's comic books and laid back on his bed. He pawed through the pages. "Oh, we had a bit of a falling out when we were kids. Money is thicker than blood and all that. That's something you should know if you're going to live in the city. It always comes down to money. With anyone. With everyone. When they sort all of us by value you're only as good as your wallet is thick. Bet your dad never thought I'd be the one to get you. I'll tell you that. He probably thought you'd go to our great aunt up in Boston. Wonder how long ago they wrote it? Must've been a couple years at least."

Randolph stood up from the bed and tossed the comic book at Bronson's feet. "I'm going to your parents' room... See if there aren't any family heirlooms your dad left lying around. You finish up in here, okay? We'll be heading for the train station shortly."

Randolph left Bronson to his task. After a few minutes

he'd put together a small pile of clothes, comics, and a few odds and ends. He scooped it all up in his arms and went to his parents' room.

Randolph stood there holding an empty pillow case picking through his mother's jewelry box. He'd take a piece out, bite it, and either toss it in the sack or on the bed. He looked up and saw Bronson.

"Done already?" he asked.

"Just taking all this junk upstairs to put in a trunk for the trip," Bronson answered, hoping his uncle wouldn't want to accompany him.

"Fine, fine. Just hurry up with it," Randolph said as he went back to sifting through the jewelry.

Bronson went to the end of the hall then lowered the door-steps to the attic. He climbed up, sat everything down at the top, then pulled the switch to turn on the light. In the back, right where it was in his vision, a sheet covered up his father's trunk. He moved the sheet then pulled the key his father had given him out of his pocket.

Bronson pushed it into the rusty lock. It clacked as it hit the tumblers... It sounded so loud he figured half the neighborhood had heard it. The lock popped open. He got down on his knees and opened the lid of the trunk.

Three throwing knifes sat on top. Bronson tested one

by throwing it into a cardboard box. Sharp. There was an orange cardboard package in a plastic baggy labeled *Necro-Fancy Flash Papers* and a bag of red tablets labeled *Wee Glimmers.* Bronson had seen his dad use the flash paper at parties but he'd never seen the Wee Glimmers before. He took one out of the bag to inspect. Nothing about it seemed all that notable. It looked like an aspirin dipped in food coloring. He tossed it over his shoulder. A loud *POP* echoed through the attic accompanied by a bright flash of light. The Wee Glimmer spun across the attic floor then sputtered out.

Bronson pulled out a brown paper package with the initials D.B. drawn in crayon. Curious, he untied the twine holding it shut then opened it up. Inside was a folded dark purple cloth. Bronson unfurled the magician's cape. Underneath that he found the most unusual item in the trunk: an old Halloween mask with faded paint but solidly built. The face on the mask reminded him of the dog that had helped him find the road. Same breed maybe? A border collie as far as he could tell. As he touched the mask. His vision filled with that strange orange glow that he'd seen in the car—

Him, on top of a building. Cape on back, mask in hand. Puts on mask. Lifts cape. Jumps. Another flash—

Bronson found himself back in the attic. He remembered his father's words.

"That is your legacy. Use it."

Bronson smiled. He snapped up his belongings then tossed them in the trunk and locked it. He grabbed the items he'd taken from the trunk then shoved them in a garbage bag he found in the corner. He climbed down the ladder back to the second floor then ran to his parents' room. Randolph snored away in his parents' bed. He walked over to the nightstand and wrote a quick note.

Uncle Randolph, I'll be back in about an hour. I just found something that I have to take to somebody from school. - Bronson

Arthur Tillman was in his backyard taking a wheel off a bike he'd "found" in a rack at the convenience several blocks from his house. It wasn't the first bike he'd "found" but it was the first one without a rusty chain. He'd been working on building his own bike for several weeks. He took a piece here, a piece there, and hoped they would all add up to a pretty sweet machine by the time he was finished.

Arthur popped the wheel off. He heard some movement from the bushes back by the garage. He picked up the wrench he'd been using then put it behind his back.

"Who's out there? You'd better come out or run back to your mommy."

Three red dots flew from the bushes. They hit the ground with a loud pop then flashed so bright it made it impossible for Arthur to see. Everywhere was light. He could only see vague shadows. One sprung from the bushes. His eyes adjusted and he saw some kid in a cape flying at him. He had a mask on... a dog maybe? The kid pulled a long dagger out from a leather sheath strapped to his ankle then waved it at Arthur.

"What... what are you thinking, kid? Put that away and go home before I kick your butt."

The kid behind the mask chuckled. "You're out kinda late," he said.

"Yeah, it's real dangerous out here at night for kids like you," Arthur said. "I destroyed kids your size when I was half your size." Arthur held out his arms then moved toward the boy. "Do I even know you?" he asked.

"Me? No, you don't know me. I'm Dogboy and I'm here to teach you not to pick on kids like me."

"Wait, I know who you are. Heard your parents died. Guess they couldn't stand having a wuss for a son."

Dogboy winced under his mask. He thought he'd done a good job disguising his voice. He'd have to practice that more later. What did Batman do? A kind of growl? That'd work.

"I am Dogboy," he said, "and I'm beating you up."

"Go home, kid," Arthur said, "I don't have time to play games with little jerks like you." Arthur took another step toward him then moved to grab the knife. Dogboy threw the knife at Arthur. It whizzed past his ear. "Big mistake, Black," Arthur said as Dogboy leapt in the air and tackled him. Before he knew what happened Dogboy's hands hit him all over his head and shoulders. He couldn't react before Dogboy was back on his feet kicking him in the stomach. What the kid lacked in upper body strength he made up for in leg strength. The kicks hit swift and hard, and they hurt. Dogboy jumped over him then landed one last kick to the back of his head. Arthur laid there shaking. He thought for sure that the little psychopath was going to kill him.

Dogboy walked over and retrieved his knife from the lawn. He slid it back into its sheath. He ran back to the bush he'd appeared from then turned back to Arthur and ripped off his mask.

"What's the matter, Tillman," he asked, "didn't see that coming?

BILL MEEKS

4

Colta City Blues

Moving day. A meeting with Principal Kane.
Cindy McNeil. Bronson helps in the AV room.

Bronson knew he was doomed the second he set foot in his uncle's apartment, but he tried to be polite.

"Interesting place, Uncle Randolph," he said.

The apartment was small. Two milk crates sat in the center of the main room. They were turned over with old pillows on top. An old portable television was propped up on a cardboard box. There were doors on either side of the room leading off to who knows where. A small half-kitchen was right next to the front door. The sink was full of dirty dishes. Some discarded junk food wrappers lay on the counter.

"You can see I'm a man of modest means," Randolph said, "which means you're going to have to contribute."

"Yeah, I can help clean the place up. Keep up on dishes. Maybe even cook. I've never done it before but I could make sandwiches and stuff."

"You misunderstand, my boy," Randolph said as he picked up Bronson's trunk, "we need money. Cash. The world doesn't spin on a satisfied mind. You can't expect me to give you a place to live *and* food, can you? I expect you'll find a job somewhere. For now let's take you to your room."

"Yes, sir," Bronson said.

He followed Randolph to the door on the left.

"Open that, would ya, Bronson?" Randolph said.

Bronson opened the door. Randolph tossed Bronson's trunk on the floor. A torn up mattress lay under a small, broken window. There wasn't much else.

"This is it?" Bronson asked.

Randolph pushed Bronson through the door. He fell on the mattress.

"You're the son of my estranged brother. You're lucky I had this much room to spare. Now get a good night's sleep. I'm required to send you to school in the morning but after that you'd better start asking around. There are a lot of shops downtown that'll let you work under the table. Think about it. G'night, my boy. Don't let me hear you breathe."

Randolph slammed the door behind him as he left. Bronson put his trunk by the window then lay down on the funky mattress and listened to the sounds of the city. Horns, sirens, and the occasional voice sent him off to sleep.

Bronson stood across the street from Woodrow Wilcox Junior High watching some kids playing hacky sack on the lawn as others made their way through the front doors. He'd arrived at the school about ten minutes prior. He hadn't worked up the gumption to go inside. He'd gone to the same schools with the same kids since kindergarten so he'd seen firsthand how new kids were treated. Heck, in his old school where he *wasn't* a new kid he didn't fare well. Encounters like the one with Arthur Tillman at the playground were not a unique occurrence.

He couldn't put off crossing the street any longer though. His Uncle Randolph told him he had to be at the school by 8 am sharp and it was 7:56. Getting to the school had been a challenge considering he'd almost never left his neighborhood on his own before but somehow he managed to navigate the city buses okay. He pulled a small mirror out of his backpack then gave himself a once over. His hair bugged him the most. There were these three big chunks that would shoot out in different directions. He pushed them back into place then crossed the street.

"Hey, new guy," a girl said as she ran up. She had an empty milk jug. "You got any pop tabs? We're collecting them for Key Club. It's for the homeless."

"What do the homeless do with pop tabs?" Bronson asked.

"I'm not sure. Maybe make clothes out of them or something? All I know is that for every one of these puppies I fill up I get a service credit toward the big party at the end of the year. So, you got any?"

"No, sorry. My mom doesn't—didn't let me drink soda."

The girl surveyed the plaza then walked over to another kid. "Hey, Carl, you got any pop tabs?"

"Yeah, my name's Bronson. What's your name? Want to be friends?" Bronson said to the spot where the girl had been standing. His first potential friend lost; he walked up the steps into the school.

Behind the desk in the front office sat an older lady. The nameplate on the desk said "Michelle Dyson - Secretary to the Principal." She wheezed as she sorted colored paper into colored stacks. Bronson walked up to the desk and waited. And waited. He coughed.

She squinted her eyes at Bronson. "You the new kid?" she asked.

"Yep," Bronson said, "Bronson Black. It's my first

day and my uncle told me I should come to the office first."

She wheeled her chair back to a waist-high filing cabinet then pulled on the bottom drawer. It didn't open. She grabbed a three-hole punch, which she used to tap the top of the cabinet a few times while jiggling the handle. "Darn thing, I've been telling him we need to replace it." The drawer shot open. She pulled out a manila envelope labeled **New Student Packet**. She handed it to Bronson.

"Take a seat over there. Principal Kane will be with you in a moment."

Bronson sat in a plastic blue chair next to a plastic green fern and thumbed through the packet. Basic stuff: map of the school, dress code guidelines (no profane language on t-shirts), club schedules. The door behind Mrs. Barnett opened. A smiling man looked in.

"Mr. Bronson Black?" the man asked.

"Yes, sir," Bronson replied.

"I'm Principal Kane," he said as he shook Bronson's hand, "Rob to my friends. Well, my adult friends. I like to think of all my students as my friends though. First off I want you to know that here at Woodrow Wilcox Junior High we pride ourselves on having a close relationship with our students. I'll tell you, Mr. Black, this city can make you ill. The other schools in the city don't care about their students. They want their pensions and enough money for a house in the suburbs. We live and breathe our students. Most of our staff live within walking distance of the school. They live in the same neighborhoods our kids do. Did you know that? We try to engage every student on a personal level. For instance, I already know a lot about you."

"Like what?" Bronson asked.

"Well, to get the negative stuff out of the way I know what happened to your parents. Awful and I'm sorry to hear it. I talked to your uncle on the phone. He seems like a good man. Very funny."

"He's okay," Bronson said.

"I also talked to your old teachers. I hear you were thinking about taking some audiovisual classes next semester, right?"

"Yeah."

"Well what do you think about taking those this semester instead? I've cleared it with Mr. Lee who runs the program and I have just the girl to help you get up to speed. They're already a month into it so I figured you'd appreciate the help."

"That sounds great, Principal Kane." It was the first bit of good news he'd had in weeks. He couldn't wait to get his hands on a camera.

"Good, well let's go meet your study buddy right now. She's a real firecracker. Her name is—"

"Miss McNeil?" Principal Kane said as he tapped a girl getting some things from her locker on the shoulder. She ducked then flipped around to face him with her fist raised.

"Yeah? Whu'da'ya want?" she said, "Oh, Principal Kane. You're looking A-MAZE-ING, as per usual. Is that a new tie?"

Principal Kane looked down at his tie with a sheepish grin. The girl took the opportunity to stick her tongue out at Bronson who stood next to him.

"Why, yes, it is. Such a nice girl." Principal Kane said. He took hold of Bronson's shoulders then guided him over to the girl. "Bronson, this is Cindy McNeil, pride of the AV room and one of my top five favorite students. Cindy, Bronson is new here today. I'd like you to show him around, let him shadow you too. I talked with Mr. Lee and Bronson is going to be joining a few of your classes. Think you can help him get up to speed?"

Cindy put her arm around Bronson's shoulder. She smiled hard at Principal Kane. "Definitely should not be a problem, sir," she said. She pulled Bronson with her down the hall. Bronson was enjoying himself as they turned the corner. She looked behind them to make sure they were out of sight then took her arm back.

"Nice to meet you, Cindy," Bronson said.

"What? Ya' gotta speak up if you want to be heard, Brandon."

"Uh... my name's Bronson."

"Bronson... Brenden... whatever." She stopped. "A few rules for getting along with me, Bronson.

47

One—I pretty much always know what I'm talking about. Two—I'm going to help you out because Big Bald Bob asked me to and I'm on his good side this week, but don't bug me too much. Can't stand people bugging me. Three— and this is the most important one— don't bug me. Ever. If I have the time to deal with you I'll let you know. If I don't let you know you don't know me. We clear?

"Yeah, we're clear," Bronson said.

"Good, now come on in and meet the boys"

Cindy opened a door marked **AV Room**. A few racks with old computer equipment lined the walls inside. Several heavy black cases were stacked in the corner. Three guys sat around a table in front of a photo backdrop of the school with the letters WWJH stenciled on it. A big camera on a dolly pointed at them. A few lights were pointed at the backdrop.

"Guys, this is Brandon," Cindy said, "Brandon, the guys."

"Bronson," he corrected.

"It's okay," said the boy with glasses and flowered shirt, "she doesn't know any of our names either."

Cindy threw her backpack against the wall then jumped up behind the camera. She reached around to the front of the camera and rotated a dial behind the lens. The door to the room opened again. A tall boy with red hair walked in. Cindy looked up from her work.

"Bugs, get out of here," she said. "I don't need you bothering my crew. We go live in five minutes."

"Nobody watches this crap, McNeil. Look at that set. I've seen better scenery in my bathroom." Bugs poked Bronson hard in the center of his chest. "Who's this geek?"

Cindy locked the camera down then ran over to them. "Bugs, don't mess with him. He's new."

Bronson winced. So much for keeping a low profile.

"Oh, a new kid, huh? Well guess that calls for a little initiation then." Bugs pushed Bronson from behind. He flew at the ground. He caught a black cable to try to break his fall. It slowed him for a second but then it gave. He fell hard on his belly. There was a loud crash. He looked up to see the

49

camera lying on the ground. The cable was attached to it. Two of the guys around the table attended to the camera. Cindy on the other hand was just about tired of the disturbance.

She grabbed Bugs's arm then twisted it behind his back.

"Aw, c'mon," Bugs said, "I was just messing around with him."

"Stay out of my newsroom, Bugs. Stay away from the kid or else." She kicked open the door then shoved Bugs into the hallway. She checked the camera for damage.

"Gee, thanks, Cindy. I could've taken him though. That was pretty awesome. The camera's ok, right?"

"You. Sit over there. Don't touch anything," Cindy said. She pointed to a chair.

"But Principal Kane said that you needed to—"

"You've been here less than five minutes and you've practically ruined my broadcast. Sit. Down. Now." Cindy said, "Before I make you." She raised her fist at him. Bronson took his bag to his spot. A heavier kid in a fedora sat next to him.

"Don't let her bother you," he said. "She takes this stuff pretty seriously but she's pretty nice once you get to know her. What was your name again?"

"Bronson."

"She'll forget about it soon, you know. The news never stops moving."

Bronson hoped so, but if the first half hour was any indication his career at Woodrow Wilcox Junior High had already reached its peak.

5

The Old Curiosity Shop

Mr. Horum makes a bad impression. Bronson stops a thief.
Parkour 101. Uncle Randolph counts his money.
Dogboy practices on the roof until the sun comes up.

That afternoon Bronson took a bus to South 4th
Street. He got off then looked around for #523. He'd
spent his lunch period in the library looking for
interesting places to go after school. When he found
the listing for The Old Curiosity Shop he knew he
had to stop. The listing he'd found promised MAGIC
TRICKS, BAUBLES, AND DO-DADS FROM THE
FAR EAST. Sounded right up his alley.

He made it to #523. The shop stood between two much larger buildings. It had a small window display with cards and trick handkerchiefs. He couldn't see inside so he wasn't even sure they were open. He heard a clap of thunder in the distance. A few drops of rain hit his head so he decided to try the door anyway.

The Old Curiosity Shop had existed in Colta City for over forty years. Its proprietor was an elderly widower of Indian descent named Mr. Horum. The shop was crowded and dusty. It smelled like the pages of an old book you'd find in the back stacks of the library. The walls were lined with shelves that themselves were packed with gags, gadgets, and gizmos (as promised). Some of the products had been there since he opened, but some had been delivered last week.

Posters, paintings, and fliers lined the walls. They showed great magicians performing their signature feats. Alexander Herrmann with his goatee and tailcoat. Across from the register Harry Kellar levitated Princess Karnak. A painting of Okito

The Mystic hung in the back. He suspended a small orange ball between his hands while clad in red oriental robes.

Mr. Horum himself stood behind the counter. He was short, chubby, and dressed like an Omani sultan. A man stood across the counter from him watching him prepare a trick. Mr. Horum placed his thumb into a miniature guillotine then slammed the blade down quick. His thumb rolled across the counter then onto the floor.

Mr. Horum chuckled as the customer jumped back to avoid the severed digit. "Is simple, hmmb?" Mr. Horum said with a smidge of pride. He held up his clenched fist, winked, then opened it to reveal that his thumb was still where it should be.

"I'll take it. How sharp is that blade?" the customer asked.

"Oh, is a bit sharp," Mr. Horum said. He took an unopened version of the trick from the shelf behind him then placed it next to the register. "...But not so very sharp. Would take off little finger at most." Mr. Horum waved his pinky at the customer. The customer chuckled then set the fake thumb up on the counter. A bell above the door sounded. Bronson walked in just in time to catch a glimpse of the thumb.

"Neat," he said.

Mr. Horum handed the trick to the customer, who tipped his hat to Bronson as he left. Bronson poked a realistic looking brain that was sitting on a table in the middle of the shop.

"And what are you needing?" Mr. Horum asked.

Bronson turned his attention to a basket with an ornate handpainted sign that said DISCOUNT GAGS—CHEAP! There were some pieces of rope, a set of trick handcuffs, and other assorted gimmicks.

"I'm looking for some good tricks," Bronson said.

Mr. Horum ducked behind the counter. "What you need?" he asked. "Card trick? Rope trick? Flash papers? We got anything you want." Mr. Horum took out several items then laid them on the counter.

"What kind of tricks can you do with rope?"

"Oh, many kinds. All sorts. Here, you like this one I betcha." Mr. Horum took a six-foot length of rope. He squinted one eye, stuck out his tongue, and took aim. He threw the rope. It spiraled through the air across the room and wrapped around a vase. It hugged the vase tighter and tighter until a small crack shot up the side of the vase, then it shattered.

"Wow," Bronson said, "but couldn't that hurt somebody?"

"It not *so* bad," Mr. Horum said, "I use trick vase."

The trick reminded Bronson of when his dad taught him how to make sugar glass. It looks like real glass, but it breaks apart easily. They'd made a piece big enough to fit in the coffee table. When his mom came home Bronson pretended to trip and fall through the "glass." He and his dad found it hilarious, but his mom didn't find it funny at all.

"Something the matter? Trick no good for you?" Mr. Horum asked.

"It's a great trick, sir," Bronson said. "Sorry. It just reminded me of a trick my dad taught me awhile ago.

"Oh, your pop do magic, hmmb?"

"He was a real magician. Traveled the country and everything."

"Well you be careful, boy-o. Your pop a magician you must have got some crazy somewhere along the way."

Mr. Horum chuckled at his joke then snatched another trick off the shelf.

"Well we need super-duper fancy trick for magician's son then." As Mr. Horum turned around he heard the bell ring above the door. Bronson was gone. He sighed, put the trick back on the shelf then went back to unpacking some marked decks.

The sun went down in Colta City. Raindrops pit-pattered on the ground like the sound of batter frying at a country fair. Water flooded into the gutters. People ran into shops or under awnings or found other places to protect them from the weather. Bronson didn't much feel like seeking shelter so he sat on the curb. The cold dirty water washed over his bare feet. He tied his shoes together then huddled around them as he let the rain wash over him.

A man barreled down the sidewalk toward him, an umbrella in one hand and a cell phone in the other. Beads of water bounced off his alligator skin shoes. He stopped next to Bronson and waited to cross the street. He looked down at Bronson, who smiled back at him. The man muttered into the phone.

"I swear, it's like Mayor Lane doesn't even care about cleaning up this city. Hand to God there's a filthy little homeless sitting in the gutter right next to me." The man bumped into Bronson as he took a couple steps past him to find a better spot to cross. An orange flash--

The man stepped off the sidewalk. Started across the road. Another man followed. Tapped him on the shoulder.

"Them's some nice shoes," he said. "Shoes like them I'd look right proper. You look like a generous sort. Care to donate to a fellow in need?"

He pulled out a small dagger. The business man backed away.

"Gladys, call 911. I'm at—"

"For Andrus," said the thief as he pushed the dagger into—

Another flash. Bronson looked on in horror as the man stepped off the curb.

"Can't they drive all the scum out of the city and be done with it?" the man said.

Bronson didn't want to help, but then he considered what happened when Spider-Man let a crook get away. He didn't think he'd mind if something happened to his uncle... but if he wanted to honor his father's legacy he needed to do something. *Might as well have a little fun with him,* he thought.

Bronson jumped up, spun his shoes around his head, then let go. They whooshed through the air, then wrapped around the man's legs. He fell, screaming, into a giant depression in the street. Bronson saw the thief from his vision run off in the other direction. He'd never even seen the man or his alligator skin shoes. The man tossed Bronson's shoes back at him.

"You just threw your whole life away, you little creep." the man said.

"I was trying to help you, ya' big jerk."

"Police! Police! Come arrest this little deviant." the man screamed. Nobody came. The man grabbed Bronson's collar. "You're going nowhere, young man."

Bronson tried to break free but the man had too tight a hold on him. He looked around. A few big, burly men stood under an awning outside a bar.

"I don't want to go with you. You aren't my dad!" Bronson screamed at the top of his lungs. The three bruisers approached the man. He let go of Bronson's collar and turned to face them.

"Now, fellas, this is all a big misunderstanding. This kid assaulted me."

As the big men closed in Bronson retrieved his shoes then slipped away. He didn't know what they'd do to the guy, but he wasn't going to stick around to find out.

By the time Bronson got close to home the rain was down to a trickle. He rounded the corner to his street and saw a group of boys taking turns climbing up the side of a building. One boy made it to the third story before climbing back down. It fascinated Bronson. He walked up to one of the boys on the ground.

"What are you guys doing?" he asked.

"Dude, it's parkour," the kid explained.

"Never heard of it," Bronson said.

"Bro, where you been?" the boy asked. "Parkour is

no joke. You learn to move around a city—up walls, over fences, rooftop to rooftop, like you'd walk down the street. Easy."

"Seems kinda dangerous," Bronson said.

"Well, yeah... but it's crazy fun too."

"How do you do it?" Bronson asked.

"Get over here and I'll show you."

He followed the boy to a set of steps next to an office building. They led to a little area with a picnic table.

"If I asked you the best way to get down to those picnic tables what would you say?"

"Go down the stairs, I guess," Bronson said, hoping that didn't sound too obvious.

"Okay," the boy said, "you ever play Tony Hawk?"

"Yeah, a few times."

"Now if I ask how you would get down to those picnic tables on Tony Hawk what would you say?"

"I guess I'd grind down the rail on the steps there, jump up to that ledge, then do a 360 down to them."

"Exactly. Now, we don't got no skateboards but it's basically the same idea. You're looking for the most natural path from A to B. Here, I'll show you."

The boy ran back about ten feet, took a few breaths, then barreled toward the steps. He jumped off the top step up onto the railing then pushed off it to jump onto the ledge. He put his hands on the ledge then did a flip off it, landing right next to the picnic table.

"See," he said, "smooth as butter." He ran back up to Bronson. "I want you to try, but there are a few things you got to remember: You got to be natural while you're doing this stuff. If it don't feel right I don't want your feet leaving the ground until it do. That means no fancy business like that flip I did unless you feel it. Okay?"

Bronson still felt a little unsure. "But what do you mean feel it?"

"You got to feel it. In every part of you, you got to feel it's right. Take your time. Feel your body. Feel your environment. When you feel it you'll know... then go for it."

Bronson stepped back to where the boy started his run. He crouched down then examined the area.

"That's right," the boy said, "figure out where you're gonna go before you do. I like to draw a little white line in my head of where I'm gonna hit."

Bronson imagined a white line tracing along the ground from his feet over the whole path the boy had taken.

"Ok, I think I'm ready," he told the boy.

"Ain't no use thinking you're ready. You got to *know* you're ready."

Bronson's leg muscles tensed. His heart beat in his chest. He moved his shoe on the still-damp pavement. And then he *knew*. He took a run at the steps then jumped from the stair to the rail to the ledge. His feet hit the ledge. He knew he wasn't ready for the flip, but he could handle another run and jump. If he rolled into it as he hit the ground he'd be alright. Run, jump, roll, then land down by the picnic tables.

"That's what I'm talking about," the boy said as ran down to Bronson.

"I did it," Bronson said. "I did it. I did it. I did it. You were right, I just felt it. Even when I realized I couldn't do the flip I kept feeling it."

"That's what parkour's all about, dude. Once you can feel it you know it."

"That was so awesome."

"No prob. Glad I could show somebody the art. Where you from, kid?"

"Around the corner here. You?"

"I live down on the West Side, but I been staying up here with my grandma because of all the stuff that's going down."

"There were some kids missing down there, weren't there?"

"My brother. Went for a field trip, never came back. "

"I'm sorry to hear that. Look, I'd love to hang out longer but I need to get home," Bronson said.

"You got it. We out here every Monday, dude."

Bronson thanked the boy and headed toward the apartment building. He couldn't believe how much fun he'd had. He almost felt like a real-life Spider-Man or something. If things went well tonight then he'd be a real-life superhero... and he couldn't be more excited.

Bronson stood outside with his ear to the door

when he got back to his uncle's apartment. He was pretty sure he didn't hear anything. He opened the door, hoping that Randolph was asleep so he could sneak to his room without talking to him.

Randolph sat on one of the egg crates in the center of the room. He sorted bills of several denominations into even, organized stacks. He looked up then went back to the money. Bronson leaned up against the wall in the corner of the room. He took a deck of his dad's cards out of his backpack. He spread them out in a line in front of him then lifted the bottom card and slid it up. The other cards stood up with it. He slid the bottom card across the tops of the other upright cards. They moved with it back and forth and back and forth several times until they fell over. Bronson pulled them back into a stack then attempted the trick again.

"Can't you do that in your room?" Randolph asked.

Bronson eyed the stacks of money. There were several stacks of one and five dollar bills, a single stack of twenties, and one small stack of fifties—a lot of money for someone who claimed he needed his orphaned nephew to find a job.

"What's your job, Uncle Randolph?" he asked.

Randolph sneered at the boy. "Keep your runny nose out of it."

"What's the big deal?"

Randolph fanned out a stack of bills.

"Bronson, there are people in this world who get it all handed to them. They leave their mom's bellies naked and cold then get wrapped up in silk sheets. I didn't have their luck."

"But my dad says you make your own luck," Bronson replied.

"Said. Your dad said. He's not saying much anymore. He didn't make his, Bronson. No, sir. Fate isn't our friend. Every once in a while it'll give you something good. Dangle it like a master might dangle a string in front of his kitten. Then the master pulls the string away, puts it in his pocket, and walks to the other room. All the kitten has left is the memory along with the sneaking suspicion that it's all for somebody else's amusement." Randolph shoved the cash in his pocket. "When I come back I don't want you out here. You have your own room.

Use it."

Bronson walked over to his room. He turned around to face his uncle.

"Why are you being like this? If my parents knew how you were—".

Randolph put a finger to his lips. "They're dead, nephew. They no longer have a say in the matter." Randolph hit the light switch then walked out the door, leaving Bronson standing in the dark.

Bronson pulled on his dog mask then opened the window in his room that led to the fire escape. He put a hand on it then pushed down hard to see if it would bear his weight. He climbed out then looked across the city. It was late but there were cars and some people walking around. Unlike his old neighborhood it seemed like every light in the city still glowed. He breathed in the scent of grilled onions filtered through his plastic mask. Not the most appetizing smell but he was getting used to it.

He ascended the fire escape, being careful not to draw the attention of other tenants in the tenement. Half the apartments seemed empty. The people in the occupied ones were either asleep or too distracted to notice him slipping past their window.

He hopped over a small ledge onto the roof. Most of the stuff in his father's trunk had been off limits to him so he needed to teach himself how to use everything. Sure, he could see into the future but just *knowing* something was about to happen might not always be enough to prevent it. He needed to make sure he was prepared for any circumstance.

The first thing he decided to work on was his hero voice. It hadn't fooled Arthur Tillman back home, and he wasn't even that smart. He pressed his vocal cords together to replicate the gravelly voice he'd used.

"I *am* the night. I *am* vengeance. *I AM DOGBOY.*"

Even though it sounded intimidating it hurt his throat a lot. It would be hard to keep up for any amount of time, and it kind of sounded pretty fake anyway. If he used it on a criminal he figured he'd get laughed at. Besides, did he want to scare people? People don't like people who scare them. No, even with the mask he was obviously a kid so he might as well use that to his advantage. No adult expects a

69

kid to beat him up or stop him from doing something he shouldn't be doing. In fact, it might work better if he tried to sound even more like a kid then he already did.

"Hi, I'm Dogboy," Dogboy said a bit higher than normal. He didn't sound exactly like himself, but if he talked to somebody who knew the real Bronson he'd know. It needed something else. He remembered his sixth grade class room where he and a few of the other kids took turns making funny voices. His friend Ryan had done a silly voice while holding his nose shut. It made him sounds stuffed up like he had a cold but also a little whiny. It didn't seem like it would be practical to run around like that though. He took a package of tissues out of his pocket then took one tissue out of the pack and ripped it in half. He took both halves then balled them up real tight. One ball went up each of his nostrils. He could still breathe out of his nose a little if he tried. They weren't too uncomfortable either.

"Hi, I'm Dogboy," Dogboy said while still making his voice a little higher. Perfect. He wanted a tape recorder to double check it at some point. To his ears he sounded like a different person.

Now to work on perfecting his knife-throwing technique. He found a stack of plywood under a tarp on the south side of the roof then propped up a few pieces along the wall. He figured he'd try to hit the targets from about ten feet. His dad always held the knife by the blade when he threw it. Dogboy did the same then took careful aim at the center board. He extended his arm then let the knife fly.

It soared through the air—blade over handle then handle over blade—but when it reached the board the handle hit it and then bounced back and landed near his feet. Undeterred Dogboy picked up the knife to try again. This time the blade hit, but it didn't stick. He tried a third time but as the knife left his hand the blade nicked his finger. He had to use another tissue from his pocket to stop the bleeding.

Dogboy held the knife up by his ear. He rocked the knife to get the feel of it. Slowly, back and forth he felt the air move around the knife... the weight of it in his fingers and shoulder. He imagined a white line between him and the board then imagined the knife leaving his hand and traveling along the line.

It felt right. He threw the knife. This time it tumbled once in the air then leveled out with the blade facing its target. It sung in a high-pitched hum as it flew through the air. The knife stabbed four inches into the board.

Dogboy walked over to the board to admire the "kill" then pulled the knife back out with a small grunt. He walked to a spot fifteen feet away to try again.

Dogboy stayed there practicing until the sun peeked out over the buildings and the sounds of the city floated up from the street below. He gathered up his things then slipped down the fire escape and back into his bedroom window. Bronson took off his costume then locked it up in the trunk. When he lay down on his mattress he found it a little more comfortable than the night before. He wasn't sure if he'd get used to it but he was too tired to care. He drifted off to sleep for an hour or so before he had to get ready for school.

6

Problems and Bigger Ones

Bugs makes out with Skyler. Bronson apologizes to Mr. Horum. Cindy interviews Mayor Lane. Randolph gives Bronson an ultimatum.

Bronson woke up to a slap in the face.

"No sleeping in the lunchroom," Cindy said. Bronson shook himself awake. Maybe late training sessions weren't the best idea on school nights. Cindy poured her carton of chocolate milk over some charcoal Salisbury steak. The sight and smell of it made Bronson want to hurl.

"On what planet is that a sensible way to put food

together?" he asked.

Cindy sopped up the milk with a biscuit. She took a big bite then smiled.

"Glad you approve, short stack." Flecks of food sprayed as she spoke.

Across the lunch room Bugs sat at a table with Skyler Weddington, one of the school's cheerleaders. Their faces inched in close to one another, meeting in a stiff kiss that was more for show than anything. There had been a lot of those around the school lately, and Cindy was sick of it.

"What's so great about kissing, anyway?" she asked nobody in particular. "I know I don't want some jerk sticking his funky tongue in my mouth."

"Yeah. Gross," Bronson said. "Kissing is *so* gross."

"So why'd you move here anyway?"

"I moved in with my uncle."

"What about your parents?"

"My parents... they died a few weeks ago."

"Sorry, kid. That's rough," Cindy said, "but at least you have your uncle."

"My dad never wanted to let me meet him. Said it wasn't a good idea. I think he was right. I mean I love the city but my uncle is... he's mean. The city's great though. You can feel how old everything is when you walk down the street."

"Look, kid, I don't even know the guy. Sorry though. That sucks."

"Thanks," Bronson replied.

They sat there and looked around the cafeteria.

"So, doing anything after school today?" Bronson asked.

"I'm working on a story," Cindy said. She stared at Skyler and Bugs with disgust.

"What about?" Bronson asked.

"You've heard of Mayor Lane? Well, he's being investigated for taking bribes from these drug companies, see? I guess there's some sort of vaccine that he let them test over on the West Side for a campaign donation or something. He says they only used volunteers in the study, but my sources tell me there's a version of the drug they were feeding in through the sewers or subways or something. I'm gonna grill him. Really put his butt to the fire, you know?"

Bronson rolled his eyes. "Like the mayor of Colta

City is ever gonna talk to a kid."

Cindy caught Bronson's ear then twisted it. "Listen up. I'm a reporter. He has to talk. It's in the constitution. I'll bet you a dollar I get him to talk."

"Jeez. Excuse me, Madame Reporter. I'll take the bet!" She let go of his ear. He picked up his tray then walked over to the old lunch lady who collected them. As he passed by the table where Bugs sat Bugs stuck his foot out— Bronson tripped right over it. He caught himself from crashing to the floor, but his tray still did. Bronson whipped around and grabbed Bugs by his shirt.

Cindy barreled across the room then jumped in between the two boys. She poked Bugs in the chest.

"Bugs, lay off the kid. Don't you know his parents died?" Bronson wished she hadn't said that. He knew kids would treat him differently if they knew. He didn't want to be known as "the kid whose parents died."

"Cindy, let it go," he said.

"No, this jerk has been a pain in my you-know-what all year. I swear to God, Bugs. If we weren't in school I'd brain you so hard."

"Oh boo-hoo," Bugs said, "he's still a walking calamity. I figure you don't want him around neither. You're too much of a gentleman to tell him yourself."

Cindy raised her fist up. Bugs laughed, threw down his books, then raised his fist back at her.

"Don't fight," Bronson asked. "He's just a big jerk anyway."

"Hey, everybody, listen," Bugs shouted to the room. "Little Orphan Bronson thinks I'm a jerk."

Principal Kane broke through the students that crowded around them. "What in heaven's name is going on here? Ms. McNeil, I expect better from you. And Mr. Black, this is no way to make a first impression." Principal Kane seized Bugs by the arm. "As for you, let's go to my office and have a heart-to-heart about your punishment. I'm sure your mother will be thrilled."

Bugs smiled at Principal Kane. "Sir, Cindy started it. I was sitting here talking to my new girlfriend Skyler, minding my own business, when she ran up and started threatening me."

"They were kissing," said a voice from the back of the crowd.

"Is that true, Miss Weddington?" Principal Kane asked.

"Yeah," she said, "but I'm *not* his girlfriend. Heather dared me to do it."

"Well, Bugs," the Principal said, "regardless of your problems with Ms. McNeil you know we have a zero tolerance policy when it comes to P.D.A. here at Woodrow Wilcox. You both need to come with me. Now."

He turned to Cindy and Bronson.

"I know you're good kids. Don't let me catch you causing trouble again or I may have to rethink that assumption. Got me?"

"Yes, Principal Kane," Cindy said.

"Got it, sir," said Bronson.

"Good," Principal Kane said, "now get to class. You kids have a newscast in an hour."

Mr. Horum stood at a display case refilling it with clown noses. A circus was in town for the next month, and he was the only shop in the whole city that carried them. The head clown came in at least a couple of times a week. The circus came through once a year and it always meant brisk business. Between the clowns and the sideshow acts the circus made up half of his business for the year. Sure, he loved demoing tricks for the random passers-by who wandered in but they weren't keeping him in business. It also gave him a chance to perform, something he didn't get to do much since his wife left. When you're the only employee it's tough to get away.

The bell above the door rang. Mr. Horum turned to greet his latest customer.

"Ah, the magician's son," he said.

Bronson looked a little embarrassed. "Yeah, sorry about the way I blew out of here the other day. I know you didn't—"

Mr. Horum ran behind the counter then pulled out a long case. "No. Is good. I figure I trick you with trick vase so you trick me back. When I turn around and you go poof I say 'Ah! This must truly be son of magician.'" Mr. Horum fiddled with the combination on the case. It clicked open. He pulled out a long sword. "No kid stuff here. I show you real expert tricks."

Mr. Horum leaned his head back then swallowed the three-foot-long sword to the hilt. Bronson smiled.

"Wicked," he said.

Mr. Horum gagged on the sword. He slid it back out quick. "No, no. Not wicked. I no do dark things. Is trick, you see?"

Bronson giggled at the old man. "I know. It's a word that means 'cool' or something like that. I know it's a trick."

"Ah, yes. You worry me for a minute you betcha. Of course a son of magician knows is just trick. You like trick, right?"

"Of course," Bronson replied.

"Well, is busy day today. Circus in town. You come back tomorrow, or other day if you like, I teach you trick and some others to boot. Good deal, hmmb? Free lessons."

"Sounds awesome, Mr.—what's your name again?"

"Horum, please to know you, magician's son."

"Bronson. My name's Bronson."

"Well, please to know you, Bronson. Tomorrow, right?"

"See you then," Bronson said as he ran out the door.

"Cindy McNeil, WWJH. I'm here to see Mayor Lane."

"WWJH?" asked the man sitting behind the front desk at Colta City Hall. "Is that new? I don't think I've ever heard of it."

Cindy pulled a rectangular piece of typing paper out of her pocket. It included a big WWJH logo and her name. She handed it to the man. "WWJH, we've won 'Best Student Broadcast' three years running."

He put the ratty business card on the ledge. "Oh, the mayor only accepts student reporters for his shadowing program."

"Yeah," Cindy said, "that's what I'm here for. To shadow him today. It's for school."

He turned to his computer and scrolled through a spreadsheet. "No shadowing scheduled for today. What's your name again? Oh, and I'll need your teacher's name too."

Cindy snatched her card off the ledge. "Wait... we had to sign up? I thought it was an open thing. Like we could just show up?"

The man pulled a white envelope from under his desk. "Here, you'll need this," he said as he offered the envelope to Cindy. "There are forms in there for you, your parents, and your teacher. And you still have to be approved, mind you."

Cindy took the envelope. "Look, I came all the way down here. I'm missing school. Can't I just go in and talk to Mayor Lane for a minute. A minute then I'm on my way."

"Young lady, we can't ask the mayor to take time out of his day every time—"

"Come on. This is so important." Cindy slammed her hands down on the ledge. "Do you realize you are the only thing standing between me and something I'll never forget? Mayor Lane is my hero. Ya' gotta."

The man looked at his spreadsheet then back to Cindy. He wound the telephone cord around his fingers then looked at Cindy, who looked pretty pitiful.

"I'll try," he said. "I'm the guy that answers the phone. I don't really have a ton of pull."

"You've got more pull than I've got, buddy," Cindy

said.

"It's Chester," the man said. He pointed to a bench in the corner of the room. "Wait over there."

Cindy nodded. She grabbed some pamphlets from a table then took a seat. Chester held his ID badge in front of a gray pad next to the door behind his desk. A red light blinked three times. A buzzer sounded. Chester went through the door, which clicked behind him.

Cindy looked through a pamphlet promoting the Colta City Library System. She counted to fifteen under her breath.

"1," she whispered.

She jumped up and bolted to Chester's desk. She opened the top middle drawer. Some Trident gum, paper clips, and a few handfuls of change. A purple nylon string ran along the bottom of the drawer and disappeared under a stack of papers. Cindy lifted up the papers. Another ID badge with Chester's picture. She scooped it up. The door behind the desk beeped. She slammed the drawer shut then jumped into her seat on the bench.

Chester walked through the door and smiled at

Cindy.

"You lucked out, honey. Mayor Lane has 15 minutes free."

Chester held the door for Cindy as she entered the mayor's study. Bookshelves lined the walls. A dark leather couch sat next to a wooden chair that sat a little higher. A white flower with three petals and a light purple center stood near the window. Cindy went over for a closer look.

"What kind of flower is this?" she asked as she reached out to touch it. A bookcase behind her creaked as it opened.

"*Lycaste virginalis*, also called the White Nun Orchid," said Mayor Lane as he emerged from the secret door. "I purchased it from a family in the Alta Verapaz province in Guatemala. It grows on the mountaintop there. I keep it here in the study where we can keep it cool. We've also set up an automatic misting system to reproduce the humidity without damaging the books. In fact, I think that's it right now."

A thin mist blew out of several hidden jets in the

wall behind the plant. The mist blew through the plant then hit Cindy in the face. She jerked back then wiped the thin layer of moisture away.

"A little warning would have been nice," she said.

"I could say the same for your visit, Miss... actually Chester didn't give me a name."

"Cindy McNeil, WWJH."

"Well, Miss McNeil with WWJH, would you care to interview me?"

Mayor Lane sat down in the chair. He gestured for Cindy to sit on the couch.

"Chester, could we have some water? Thirsty day today."

"I'm not that thirsty," Cindy said. She sat down.

"No, young lady," the mayor said. "You're my guest. I insist."

Chester left then returned a moment later with a two glasses of water. The ice cubes were small and brittle. Sweat dripped down the sides of the glasses. Cindy politely took a sip.

Mayor Lane grabbed his glass. "Now," he said, "Cindy, was it?"

Cindy nodded.

"Cindy, what do you want to know?"

"Mayor Lane, is the rise in misdemeanor thefts around the city a temporary spike, or do you think there's more to it?"

Mayor Lane chuckled. "What? Are you asking if I believe the ghost stories about a man organizing the small-timers? The Guild of Thieves? Absolutely not. We are setting record high temperatures. Our welfare bill is higher than it's ever been, as is unemployment. The spike, and that's all it is, the spike in crime in Colta City is easy to explain. Most importantly it was expected. Our fine Colta City PD is prepared to face this perfectly normal spike in activity. Most students start with 'What does the mayor do?' by the way. Good to see one of you who has an interest in current events."

"Yeah," Cindy said, "I gotcha. Yeah. Now I had a question about the... West—" Cindy's eyes closed. She fell over on to the couch. Her water spilled on the carpet. Mayor Lane sat his water on the end table.

"Chester," he called, "I might need a hand here."

Bronson sat on his mattress shoving some tuna and crackers in his mouth as he worked on his homework for TV class. He was trying to find a way to make that afternoon's student council meeting interesting for the next day's edition of WWJH News. They'd talked about decorating the halls for the spring fling. Bronson figured they might as well call themselves the social council instead of the student council. It would be more accurate.

As he shoved the last few crackers into his mouth the door to his room slammed open. Randolph stood on the other side. He shoved Bronson back into the room. Bronson crawled back over to the wall. He'd seen his uncle flippant, annoyed, even happy... never angry like this.

Randolph held up an empty tuna tin. "I thought I made it clear that my food is mine. You don't touch it," he said. He paced back and forth a few times then chucked the empty can at the wall next to Bronson's head. "Just because you're living here it doesn't mean you have permission to use whatever you'd like."

"But I gotta eat, don't I?" Bronson asked.

"What did I tell you when you first moved in? I said you were going to have to contribute. Eating my food is *not* contributing. It's stealing, and nobody likes a thief. Trust me. I'll bet you haven't even thought about looking for a job yet."

Bronson realized at that moment he hadn't. He'd been so busy with school and his training it hadn't occurred to him.

"I'm sorry, Uncle Randolph. I'll look tomorrow."

"You'd better. Or you won't be coming back here anymore. Word to the wise: I hear the fine citizens of Colta City treat street kids less than kind. You should think about selling some of your things." Randolph jiggled the padlock on Bronson's trunk.

"Don't touch that, it's mine," Bronson said.

"Why is it locked?" Randolph asked. "What are you hiding in there?"

"Nothing," Bronson said. He held the door open for his uncle. "It's all my old junk. Comics and clothes. I just keep it locked in case somebody breaks in or something."

"Looks like your dad's. Did he leave you something, Bronson? Holding out on your old uncle, are you?"

"Just the trunk. I swear."

Randolph tugged on the lock. "If you can find a buyer it might buy you a few more nights. The hunt begins tomorrow, nephew. Knock 'em dead."

7

The Cowboy in the Parking Garage

A vision in the parking garage. The Cowboy.
Bronson writes a letter. Blaze gets grilled.

Bronson set everything he would need for that night's patrol out in front of him: a pile of Wee Glimmers, some Necro-Fancy Flash Papers, a throwing knife, the cape, and his mask. He heard some footsteps out in the living room. The front door to the apartment shut. He balled up some tissues and put them up his nostrils. He bowed his head and slipped the mask over it. He carefully eased it over the tip-top of his head lest it rip and leave him without a disguise. He tied the cape around his neck, placed the dagger in its sheath around his ankle, and placed the Wee Glimmers and flash paper in the cargo pocket of his shorts. He locked the trunk to keep his uncle from snooping, opened the window, and ascended the stairs up to the roof of the building.

He didn't quite understand why superheroes always traveled by rooftop. For somebody like Spider-Man it made sense, but Batman or Daredevil? Why introduce another element of danger to an already dangerous job? Maybe they felt like fewer people would see them? Regardless, it was tradition and if Dogboy was going to be an actual superhero he figured he needed to get used to it.

He walked to the center of the rooftop and looked across the way to the parking garage next door. He traced a white line across the rooftop to a spot about three feet from the ledge then over the ledge and across to the parking garage. He took a moment to "feel it" like the parkour kid had told him to the other day. He took a few deep breaths and felt everything click. He ran as fast as he could along the rooftop. When he hit the spot he jumped up to the ledge, crouching down as he landed to absorb the impact. He bounced back up and flew off the edge. He looked down at the alley below and realized just how high up he was. The cement wall of the parking garage came into his field of view and he realized he hadn't prepared for his role at all. He brought his knees to his chest and skidded as he hit the pavement, his calf scraping along the cold cement. As he came to a stop he winced, but it didn't look that bad. His calf was scraped, but it wasn't any worse than the rug burn he'd received playing soldier in the living room when he was nine.

He was happy he'd made it but decided maybe he'd had enough of rooftops for one night. Best to ease into it. He saw a stairwell on the other side and decided to head down.

Dogboy sprinted down the stairs. As he hit level four his vision went orange. He thought it was weird. He'd never had a "flash forward" as he'd taken to calling them without coming into contact with somebody before. He figured either his power was getting stronger or he was having a brain hemorrhage. He saw a woman back up against a brick wall. The sign next to her said **Level 3**. The woman screamed. The silhouette of somebody in a cowboy hat covered her.

And then the vision was gone. Dogboy was pretty sure it was the same parking garage he was in. It had looked similar anyway. It had to be close for his power to kick in like that, right? He crept down the steps and opened up the door to the third level. It creaked on its hinges. He froze. He peeked out the door. Nobody seemed to be around. He stepped out and looked to his left. The sign from his vision was there next to him.

He decided the best thing he could do was wait. But he couldn't wait out in the open. He might alert the crook and miss his first opportunity at a real superhero adventure. There was a powder blue town car parked a few feet away from the door. He tiptoed over and tried the door handle. Locked. He lay down on the ground and rolled under the car. The dirty concrete floor didn't do his already scraped leg any favors. He reached down and took the knife from its sheath then waited for the night to really begin.

Jody O'Leary was tired. She was supposed to leave the office hours ago but a client in London often "forgot" about the time difference. Conference calls usually sucked the life out of her, but this one had been beleaguering. She opened the door on the third floor of the parking garage (where she was pretty sure she'd parked) and looked around for her car as she dug through her purse for her keys.

She spotted the car right away, but her keys were harder to find. She dug deep underneath the foundation and empty packs of gum but she still couldn't find them. "Oh my God," she said. "If I left them in the office I am going to freak."

Bronson had only slept a few hours the night before so it wasn't surprising that he was fast asleep under the car. A puddle of drool pooled on the pavement. A women's voice startled him awake and he jerked his head up to look around. It smacked off the oil filter but he caught himself before he could scream. He looked out from under the car and saw a pair of modest heels standing just a few feet away from him. This was it. He just had to wait a little longer for the bad guy to show up.

Jody was so busy looking for her keys that she didn't see the man step out from behind the minivan parked a few cars down. She didn't notice his shining white boots, his string tie, or his ten-gallon hat. She didn't see him mosey toward her while he chewed on a piece of straw. But then she noticed, and it gave her a start. She jumped. Held her hand to her chest and laughed.

"Oh," she said. "You scared me. Quite an outfit you've got there, cowboy."

He smiled and tipped his hat.

"Name's Blaze, darling. Beg your pardon. Do you need some help?"

Jody clawed through her bag for her keys.

"No," she said, "I'm fine. Just looking for my phone. Have a good night."

Blaze took hold of the hand she was using to dig for her keys and placed his other hand over it.

"Shame for a pretty little thing like you to be all alone out here. Give me your bag and I'll help you find whatever it is you're looking for." He dropped the smile.

"Sir, you are making me very uncomfortable," Jody said as she pulled her hand out his grasp. "I'm leaving. Okay. I don't need any—"

"Ma'am, tweren't a request. Don't put up a fight. You'll make me sorry for not turning out the lights."

Blaze pulled a small pistol from the holster on his hip. Jody had assumed it was all part of the costume but now she was pretty certain it was an actual firearm. She backed up toward the door and felt behind her for the doorknob. He advanced on her until she was up against the wall. She tried to push out a scream but all that came out was a chirp. He put his finger up to her lips and shushed her.

Dogboy peeked out from underneath the car and got a look at the guy. Man, was he tall. And big. Dogboy thought it might be best to startle Blaze before showing himself. If he just jumped out from under the car the guy would have a few seconds to get the jump on him. He pulled the flash papers and a lighter from his pocket. He reached out and slid a few pieces of the paper under Blaze's boot.

Blaze reached out and touched the women's cheek. She looked away and her lip quivered. "Aw, don't you frown," he said. "You sure are pretty. Let's go down and spend a night in the city." As he leaned in for a kiss he smelled something burning. Black smoke drifted up through his mustache and into his eyes. He looked down. His boot was on fire. He jumped back and hooped and hollered and tried to stomp it out.

Dogboy stabbed his throwing knife into Blaze's leg from underneath the car. Blaze screamed and fell over onto the ground. He turned his head and saw Dogboy underneath the car.

"What in tarnation?" he said.

Dogboy rolled out from underneath the opposite side of the car. Blaze's fingers dug into his ankle. He tried to pull loose but Blaze had a pretty good grip on him.

"Gotcha now, ya' little rascal."

Dogboy took his free foot and kicked at Blaze's hand. He took hold of the body of the car with both hands and pulled. His last kick loosened Blaze's hold and he wiggled his way out from underneath the car. He jumped up and ran around to the other side.

"You okay, ma'am?" he asked Jody.

By this point Blaze was up on his feet. He moved in toward Dogboy and Jody until he saw that Dogboy still had a knife in his hand.

"Don't you folks worry. I guh-got the point. I'm in a hurry to get out of this joint." Blaze turned and limped across the parking garage and out the door on the other side.

Dogboy turned around to Jody, who was still up against the wall clutching her purse.

"Hi there, lady," Dogboy said with a huge smile hiding behind his mask, "Tell the world this crook has paid thanks to 'The Amazing Dogboy.'"

Dogboy took a bow as Jody looked at him incredulously.

"You let him get away," she said. "I wouldn't call that 'amazing'"

"How about 'fantastic'?"

Jody shook her head as she plucked her keys out of her bag and headed toward her car. "You know what, kid. I'll give you 'fantabulous,'" she said.

Dogboy thought it over. "That'll work," he said.

She turned around. "What's a kid your age doing out this late anyway?"

"Um... sightseeing?" Dogboy said.

"In a parking garage?" she asked.

Dogboy shrugged. He pulled some Wee Glimmers from his pocket. "It's been fun saving you, and remember..." He threw the Wee Glimmers against the ground and they exploded in a flash of light. Jody shielded her eyes as his voice echoed through the structure saying "I. Am. Dogboy."

Jody looked back and saw that Dogboy was gone. Then she noticed some movement underneath the blue car.

"I can still see you, kid," she said.

"Aw, nuts," came Dogboy's voice from underneath the car.

Blaze sat in subway tunnel as a train blew by him. He held onto his hat so it wouldn't blow off his head. He was avoiding going back to where he slept. Andrus wouldn't be happy. It was one thing to botch a robbery. It happened to old timers and newbies alike almost every night. It was another thing to have his hat handed to him by some kid playing dress up.

There was no avoiding it though. The sun was coming up and that meant he needed to get underground. With the way Mayor Lane was cracking down it wasn't safe to be out during daylight hours. For all he knew every cop in Colta City had his picture. It's not like he tried to fade into the shadows either. The other guys made fun of his whole cowboy motif but he liked it. It reminded him of his life before the Guild.

He'd been a performer in a show at Curleyworld on the outskirts of the city. Once an hour he and a dozen other guys would emerge from the saloon in the Old California section of the park and have a shootout for about fifteen minutes. Families who'd come up to him after the show always told him he had the best death scream. It was a good job, and he was sorry he'd lost it. He'd found a key in the maintenance room that opened up the guest lockers people locked their valuables in at the entrance to the park. It wasn't like he was taking people's stuff that they were depending on. No, he'd go in after the park had emptied out and take anything that they'd left behind. It was never much. A wad of bills here. A gold ring there. But they caught him. He did keep his spare costume though.

He'd holed up in his apartment after that, but when he ran out of money his landlord called the cops. His first days on the street were hard. The soup kitchens ran out of food fast and the homeless shelters filled up even faster. He'd sleep behind a dumpster on 15th Street during the day and wander around at night asking random strangers for change so he could go to the all-night 7-11 and grab a couple taquitos. He did pretty well with his costume and cowboy shtick, but as the costume got dirtier and he got smellier the "donations" began to dry up. It was a middling existence, and lonesome.

When winter came, living on the streets became unbearable. One night it got so cold he even risked going down into a subway station for a couple of hours so he could get feeling back in his toes. He was hopeful he could stay under the cop's radar that long.

He was sitting on a bench out of the way of most of the foot traffic when he saw another homeless man walk to the edge of the platform, look around, then jump down onto the tracks. He followed him since he figured he might know something. And that was the night he met Andrus and his life changed.

But he didn't want to face Andrus now. He was ashamed of what had happened but he knew he had to tell him. Andrus didn't seem to be bothered by cops interfering with the Guild's work, but if there was some kid out there playing superhero he'd want to know. He hoped that Andrus's reaction wouldn't be too severe. Andrus wasn't kind when he wasn't happy. As he wandered down the subway tunnel he hoped that the information he had would outweigh the news of his defeat.

Bronson crawled back in his window and placed his costume back in his trunk. He laid down on his mattress and watched the city lights outside of his window. He played the scene of him taking down the cowboy over and over in his head. He couldn't believe he stopped a crook. Sure, he'd escaped but that just meant they were bound to face off again another day. Maybe Blaze would become his arch nemesis. He knew he'd have one eventually. Every hero does.

He sat up and dug around in his trunk. He pulled out a composition notebook hidden in one of the side flaps and flipped it open a few pages. He'd started writing his parents letters. Sure, they'd never read them but he thought it would make him feel a little better and he had to tell somebody about what happened that night.

Dear Mom and Dad,

The reason I'm writing you is to let you know that I found the trunk. The mask. The tricks. Everything. It's a superhero outfit, right? I hope so because that's what I'm using it for. Dad, did Mom know you were giving me this? I bet she didn't. She would have never let you give me real knives. And the whole "seeing into the future" thing... Have you been able to do that forever? I wish you'd been able to stick around a little longer to tell me how it works. I wish you'd both stuck around a little longer in general. I miss you guys.

So, anyway, the trunk. I went out on my first

adventure tonight. I saved a lady from a guy who was dressed up like a cowboy. How crazy is that? It was kind of a cheesy costume. Kind of like in those old Roy Rogers movies you tried to get me to like. Anyway, I stabbed him in the leg. Just a little, though, don't worry. And he was going to attack her or something. I had to. I did pretty good though. She even thanked me.

Well, I just wanted to let you guys know about all that. I miss you. If anything about this power means you can come back, do it. I don't even care if you guys are zombies or something. I just want to see you again. I love you.

-Bronson

Andrus sat in the corner of the dark room watching Blaze squirm under the light. He was a thin man, unremarkable apart from the black hood and top hat he wore. Blaze had come back empty handed, which was a big no-no even for somebody Andrus trusted as much as he trusted Blaze. In the short time Blaze had been in the Guild he'd proved invaluable and often brought in more than a dozen other men combined. His appearance allowed him to get close to his marks before they suspected a thing.

"You've done wrong by the Guild tonight," Andrus said. "Some of your brothers will go hungry. What happened out there?"

Blaze took off his hat and placed it over his chest. His hands were shaking, which pleased Andrus. He preferred his men to have a healthy fear of him. "I'm sorry," Blaze said. "I done got caught."

Andrus gripped Blaze's hair and yanked his head back. "The police? You know you're supposed to stay away from here for at least a week if they catch you. You've compromised every one of your brothers."

"It wasn't a cop who popped me," Blaze said.

Andrus let go of his hair. "Well, then who was it? One of your marks?"

"It was some little punk, tweren't coulda been more than fifteen or so I reckon."

Andrus laughed. "A child? You were caught by a child? If I was you I would have lied and said it was a large man, but nobody would lie about a child. A child? Amazing."

"He got the drop on me while I wasn't lookin',

Andrus. Stabbed me in the leg. He was wearing some weird get-up too. Looked like a dog."

Andrus returned to his desk. "A dog you say?" he asked.

"Yes, sir," replied Blaze.

"Ah, well. How were you to know? We'll do better tomorrow night, won't we?"

Blaze put on his hat, stood, and smiled. "I reckon," he said, "and if I see that kid again I'll whip him like the mutt he is."

"Now don't be too hasty. Why don't you bring Hot John and Professor Osbert in here. I think we might be able to make use of this dog boy."

8

Andrus and the Guild of Thieves

Bronson gets a job. Cindy wakes up below City Hall.
Andrus makes a speech to the guild. Cindy talks to her mom.
Uncle Randolph does a mean thing.

Bronson was surprised Mr. Horum had let him behind the counter. He always thought there would be some sort of special pass or something you'd need to get behind the counter at a store. But when you were the personal guest of the owner he supposed that was the only pass you needed.

Mr. Horum placed a deck of cards on the counter in front of Bronson. "This expert deck. It called

Svengali deck. Well, not a deck for experts. It make anybody look like expert though. Does many tricks. You pick up, Bronson."

Bronson picked up the deck.

"Now, you see any funny business there?" Mr. Horum asked.

Bronson flipped through the deck a couple of times. It seemed pretty normal. He tapped it on the counter and noticed something. "Some of the cards are shorter than the others," he told Mr. Horum.

"Aha! You see the trick. Pretty simple, hmmb? This is why you can never let them hold the deck. Too easy to spot. But easy to do tricks with too. See, short cards are all same card. Watch. I flip through cards and you tell me stop."

Mr. Horum held the deck with the cards facing toward Bronson and began to flip through them.

"Stop," Bronson said.

Mr. Horum stopped. The card left standing was the queen of clubs.

"You take," Mr. Horum said.

Bronson took the card. Mr. Horum held the deck face down out to Bronson.

"You put card anywhere you want. Sky the limit," Mr. Horum said. Bronson chose a spot about three-fourths of the way through the deck. Mr. Horum picked the deck back up and shuffled it.

"Nice thing about Svengali deck is deck does trick for you." He dropped the deck on the table. "Now, you see what top card is."

Bronson picked up the top card and sure enough it was the queen of clubs. "Wow, that's a pretty good trick," he said.

"You take deck and practice. Show friends at school. And tell them where you get it."

"Aw, thanks, Mr. Horum," Bronson said.

"Anything for magician's son," Mr. Horum said as he tussled Bronson's hair. "You get to school now, yes?"

"Say," Bronson said, "you wouldn't be hiring, would'ya? My uncle wants me to find a job."

Mr. Horum took off his glasses. He gave Bronson a stern look. "Ah. Now I see, hmmb? Cards not good enough. Lessons not good enough. You want Horum's money." Bronson was concerned he'd offended his new friend, but then Mr. Horum shot him a wink and he knew he was just messing with him.

"Kinda, yeah," Bronson said.

"This I can do. Come tomorrow. Three o'clock. I fix you up."

"AM or PM?" Bronson asked. It didn't matter to him, he was usually up at either time. The AM shift might cut into his crime fighting though.

Mr. Horum put his glasses back on and started stocking a display. "No boy up and out at three AM. Of course PM. And dress nice."

Bronson looked down at his smudged shorts and realized how scrubby he was starting to look. He had a couple nice outfits left he hadn't worn yet, but maybe once he started making some money he could at least afford a trip to the laundromat. "You got it," he said as he ran out the door.

Mr. Horum chuckled to himself. "Oh, I pay for this, you betcha," he said.

"Hey, girl, you okay?"

The voice woke Cindy up. The room she was in was windowless. There were a few plants that gave off a soft green light. A boy sat in the corner across from her. He was around her age and wore pajama bottoms and a plain white t-shirt.

"Girl, you gonna make it?" he asked.

Cindy sat up. "Where am I? How long was I out?"

"They brought you in a few hours ago. No idea how long you've been here. They like to ship us around a lot."

"Us?" Cindy asked. "Are there other kids here?"

"Yeah. A lot actually."

"Last thing I remember I was talking to the mayor," she said.

"Shadow program?" the boy asked.

"Yeah, I guess."

"Shadow program means you don't never see your shadow again. That's how we all ended up here."

"Where is here?" Cindy asked.

"Secret base? Prison? I don't know. They don't let us see out. For all I know we got abducted by aliens or something."

"How long have you been here?" Cindy asked.

"A week or something. Kinda hard to tell without knowing when it's daylight out. Only light we get are the plants and the little red eye over there." The boy pointed to a gray plate near the door.

Cindy reached into her pocket and pulled out the ID badge she'd lifted from Chester's desk.

"Hey, I think I can get us out of here," she said.

"Tried that my first day. Trust me, you don't want them catching you."

"You don't want to come?"

"Oh, I'll get out of here when I'm sure I can stay out of here. It'll make the news when I get out of here. I'm taking these suckers out. Truth."

Cindy scanned the ID card. The light flashed, the beep beeped, and the door clicked open.

"Well, good luck with that and everything. I'm Cindy by the way."

"Axle," the boy said.

"Good luck, Axle." Cindy walked through the door and closed it shut behind her.

The hallway outside the room was as dark as the room itself. Cindy felt along the wall for a light switch. She felt two small round buttons stacked vertically. The bottom one was pushed in. Cindy pushed the top button. The wall shook then opened.

An open service elevator descended and stopped in front of her. A small light turned on inside it.

Cindy opened the accordion gate and stepped onto the elevator. There were three buttons: ML, TL, and LL. Cindy pressed ML and the walls fell away. The elevator shook as it went up. It stopped in front of a large wooden door. There was an ID scanner. Cindy scanned the stolen ID and the door clicked opened. She rolled a fist with one hand and put the other on the door. She took a deep breath and pushed the door open. She froze as the man in the room turned toward the open door.

ML didn't stand for "main level" like she'd assumed. It stood for Mayor Lane and went directly to his study by way of the bookcase.

"Miss McNeil, how did you get in there? Well, Chester will just have to take you back down."

"I'm not going back down there, you creep." Cindy grabbed a thick book off one of the shelves and threw it at the Mayor. Mayor Lane ducked. The book flew past him and crashed into the rare orchid placed near the window. It fell to the ground. The book landed on top of the flower and crushed it flat.

Mayor Lane grabbed Cindy and pushed her back to the elevator.

"You will regret that, Cindy," Mayor Lane said, "and you are going back down there. Right now. And you'll never get out again."

Cindy grabbed the mayor's hands and tried to loosen his grip.

"Let me go. Please, Mayor, I just want to go home. I won't tell anybody anything I swear. Just forget I was ever here. Let me go home."

Mayor Lane let go of Cindy and held up his hands.

"Young lady," he said, "why would I stop you from going home? How did you get in here anyway? Wander off from a tour group?"

"I... yes, that's exactly what I did." Cindy walked toward the office door. "I'd better go find them. Nice meeting you, Mayor."

"You too, young lady. Do you want a picture before you go?"

Cindy smiled as she backed up toward the door.

"Aw, thanks. I don't have a camera though."

Cindy waved at the mayor and walked out the door.

She took a few quick steps down the hall. There was an exit sign over a door at the end of the hallway. She ran to it and pushed it open. A shrieking alarm sounded. Cindy ignored it and ran down the alley as police sirens approached from the station a few blocks away.

The cavern was dark and dank, save for a few work lights that reflected off the ceiling. The walls were concrete but they met loose earth about halfway down. In front stood a bare stage put together with scrap pieces of plywood and random discolored boards. It was large enough to hold a dozen men, but it looked strong enough to hold three or four at the most. Discarded train seats were lined up in rows like pews in a church. They were filled with men who looked and smelled like they'd seen better days. A woman in a junky coat took a swig of a brown liquid from an unmarked bottle. She burped without apology and stared at the man sitting next to her.

"I'll tell you something, buddy," she said, "I think—" And then she fell over and began to snore.

The man she'd been talking to jumped up and started going through her pockets. Some people across the room noticed and came over to grab her shoes. One snapped up the bottle. As he took a drink he felt a tap on his shoulder.

"Gentlemen," said Andrus, "how are we to accomplish anything if we betray each other? Help Sister Francine into her seat. And you, go take care of her son while she sleeps it off."

"Sorry, boss," the man said. He and the other people who'd been picking Sister Francine clean lifted her up and tossed her onto an empty train bench.

The room went dark and the gathered thieves made their way to their seats. Andrus stepped on the stage. The room remained quiet as he looked out over his brothers. They dare not make a sound until he was ready for them to. They had seen on many occasions what would happen if they did that. It wasn't a violent punishment, but it was cruel. Speak before Andrus was ready for you to speak and you were escorted out of the underworld and never allowed to return.

"The people above us do not care if we survive," Andrus said. "They sit in their new houses with their old money and ask that we, the hopeless, be thrown in cages when we dare ask for a loaf of bread. Yet, they live in cages. They spend thousands of dollars on devices meant to protect them from men like us who didn't have the luck to be born into wealth. The men they spit upon when they walk into the bank."

"God didn't give us what they have. But fear not. Now we stand together and take what they have because after years of being trampled and put upon and kicked around *we* are the ones who deserve it." Andrus raised his hands and the room erupted in applause and cheers.

"We are the Guild of Thieves, and we exist to take back this world from the rich and the powerful. In ancient times kingdoms were run by kings and fought for by people like us. And what has changed? The kings are now called hedge fund managers and the battlefields are the unemployment lines. The rich are richer, the poor are poorer, and evil men live above while good men live below. No more. Soon we arrest this regression and push humanity toward a brighter path. That is our destiny."

"But," Andrus continued, "some men would like to take our destiny away from us. A boy dressed as a dog hurt one of us, and by hurting one of us he has hurt all of us."

Sister Francine, awakened from her sleep by the cheers, stood up and held her bottle over her head. "Where is 'ee? I'll take his eyes out and we can play some marbles." The crowd roared in approval.

"Do not harm him," Andrus screamed over the din of the crowd. "If you encounter him, watch him. Play with him. Find out what he can do and what he knows. Do not fear him. Who has protected you?"

"Andrus!" screamed the thieves.

"Who has fed you and clothed you?"

"Andrus!" the thieves said again.

The lights shut off as the crowd continued to chant Andrus's name, and when the lights came back on, their leader was gone.

"ANDRUS! ANDRUS! ANDRUS!" they continued well into the night.

Tess huffed as she pulled the kitchen stove out

from the wall. She beat at the thick layer of dust on the floor with her broom until the air was soupy. Her cell phone speakers blasted out the sound of a laughing chipmunk. She squeezed past the stove and grabbed the phone off the counter.

"Miss McNeil?" the operator said.

"This is Tess McNeil."

"Miss McNeil, this is Sergeant Martin with the Colta City Police Department. Are you decent? Officer Link should be there in just a moment."

"You found her?" Tess asked.

"The officer should be there, ma'am. Go to the door."

Tess wobbled across the fresh-swept kitchen floor toward the front door. The room got longer with every step she took. A dull thump came from the front door. And another. Every step took fifteen years and every breath took a century. She grabbed the doorknob and turned it.

The door flew open. A cyclone flew past her and plopped down on the couch.

"Hey, Mom," Cindy said, "what's shaking?"

Tess ran over and grabbed Cindy by the

shoulders.

"Where have you been? Do you have any? I was. I was just. Cindy. I-- Why? Are you ok? Where did you go?"

The officer outside the door coughed. "Ma'am, I take it this is the right house. Her picture came over the computer a few hours back. Saw her strolling around at the corner of Fox Trot and Fincastle. Almost made it back herself."

Tess hugged Cindy tight. "Where were you?" she asked.

Cindy hugged her mom back and looked at Office Link in the doorway.

"Can we talk about it after we lose the narc, Mom?" Cindy asked.

Tess rushed over to the door. "I'm sorry, officer. She didn't mean any offense by it. Is it possible that we could have some time to talk as a family?"

"I get it, ma'am," Officer Link said as she took a step back. "It isn't exactly by-the-book, but I'm willing to leave you two to talk. I spoke with your daughter in the car. Smart girl. Said nobody hurt her. You can call the station if she tells you anything else. Have a good night, ma'am."

"Thank you for making an exception, officer," Tess said. "Tell you what... stop on down at Erin's Pub some night after your shift and your drink's on me." Officer Link tipped her hat and turned to walk to her car. Tess closed the front door.

Cindy's kicked her shoes off on the floor. She lay across the couch hugging a pillow with her eyes closed.

"Nice try, kiddo," Tess said. "Up. Now."

"Ah, Mom. I'm exhausted," Cindy said. Tess patted her legs. She sat up.

"You've been gone a full day. Do you know how worried I've been? I had to call off too. Can't wait to deal with *that* tonight, by the way. Your butt isn't leaving this couch until I get some answers. Now where were you?"

"I don't want to say." Cindy hugged her pillow tighter.

"Now, Cindy or you don't get to intern at the TV station like you wanted."

Cindy jumped up. "You can't do that. WRDB isn't just a TV station. They're the biggest station in the state. You wouldn't."

"I'm serious, young lady. If you care about it that much you'd better start spilling."

Cindy looked up at her mom. She grabbed her and gave her a hug. "Mom, it was awful. They put me in this basement with a bunch of other kids and I didn't know what to do."

Tess pulled Cindy back and looked at her face. "Who? Who took you? Did they hurt you?"

Cindy grabbed a tissue from the box on the coffee table and blew her nose. "You'd never believe me."

"Try me," Tess said.

"The mayor. Mayor Lane. I went to interview him and I don't think he liked my questions."

"The mayor? What were you doing interviewing the mayor?"

"Mom, I—" Cindy took her mother's hand, "I don't want you to worry about this, ok? I made it out. Nobody hurt me. They gave me some drugs or something but I feel fine. Don't worry about it. Forget about it. It's not important."

Tess stared at her daughter for a little longer than was comfortable then smiled and walked toward the kitchen. "I'm just glad you're home, dear. I'll grab you a little snack and then you can take a nap. I have work in a couple hours, ok? Anything special you want for dinner?"

"Pizza?" Cindy asked.

"Pizza," Tess replied. "And next time call if you're planning on pulling an all-nighter for school."

"No prob, Mom," Cindy said.

Tess went into the kitchen. Cindy lay down and closed her eyes. She felt guilty but figured it was for the best. If she hadn't done it her mom would worry, and Cindy figured she's probably be doing enough worrying for the both of them.

Bronson slept on the floor in the blue glow of the small television set. An action sting rang from the TV. An announcer said, "Police remain helpless as muggings, carjackings, and assaults continue to rise in Colta City. Is crime on the rise, or is there something more sinister going on? Tune in to News Channel 67 at 11 and find out."

Bronson heard the sound of keys in the door. He hadn't expected his uncle to come back this early, if at all. He'd learned over the course of the past couple of weeks it was usually safe to hang out in the middle room past ten o'clock. The door opened. He closed his eyes and pretended to be asleep.

"Welcome to the old homestead, m'love," Randolph said to the less-than-honorable girl he escorted inside the apartment. He saw Bronson curled up on the floor.

"Who's the kid?" she asked.

"Oh, him? An intruder I'd assume. Why don't you be a good girl and wait in the hall a moment and I'll dispose of him. Won't be a second, love."

"Okie-dokie, Randy," she said, "but don't leave me waiting too long." She stepped out and Randolph closed the door behind her.

He walked over to where Bronson was sleeping and pulled him up on his feet by the scruff of his shirt. The collar tightened around his neck and he gagged. He decided playing dead was probably his best option. He rolled his eyes back in his head and pretended he weighed a thousand pounds.

"I thought I tol' you to stay in your room, boy," Randolph said.

"I was just watching TV," Bronson said.

"Don't play dumb," Randolph said as he dropped Bronson. "You know that room over there is yours. The rest of the apartment is mine. Speaking of... you got my money?"

Mr. Horum had just paid Bronson his fifty-five dollars for the week that afternoon. He'd bought some food that he'd hidden in his room and done a load of laundry down at the corner laundromat. That left him with about $35 for the next week. He pulled a twenty dollar bill from his pocket and held it out to his uncle.

Randolph snatched it out of his hand and inspected it. "I thought you were making good money at that magic shop. Where's the rest?"

"Well I picked up some food and stuff," Bronson said. "You said I should do that, right?"

"We had a simple arrangement. You give me money and stay out of my way and you have a place to sleep." Randolph put his hand on Bronson's shoulder. "You have no respect for our arrangement, kid." He yanked Bronson by the hair and dragged him over to his door. He opened the door and threw

Bronson in. "I'll be back in the morning. If you're still here I'll be happy to reunite you with your parents. You're a freeloader, kid. Let's see how you like it when you don't have anybody to mooch off anymore."

"But... but I don't have anywhere else to go," Bronson said.

"And for good reason I say," Randolph said. "Who would want you?"

9

The Guild Strikes!

Bronson finds a hideout. Cindy and Bronson return to school.
Sister Francine. The good guys get cornered in the magic shop.

Bronson stopped and sat on his trunk for a few minutes to catch his breath. He'd been lugging it around with him all day while he looked for somewhere to sleep. Every time he thought he'd found a safe place to set up shop somebody would show up and tell him to beat it or he'd see a cop and get nervous. It was almost time for him to be at work, and if there was anything he needed if he was going to make it on the streets it was money. From taking the trash out every day at the end of his shift he knew that there was a relatively private alleyway behind The Old Curiosity Shop where he could stash his trunk until his shift was over.

When he reached the alley he took a quick look around and pulled the trunk back. There was a large green dumpster that would hide it from the street until he was done. He pulled the trunk around and pushed it behind the dumpster. A few rats scurried out. He hoped they'd leave it alone since he had some packs of crackers in it. Could rats chew through a trunk like this?

He noticed the wall was missing some bricks. The hole was big enough that the trunk would fit in it or at least it would if he knocked a couple more out. He wiggled behind the dumpster and leaned down to look inside. To his surprise there was a large opening through the hole, at least as big as his room back at Uncle Randolph's place. Lying right inside were the bricks that were missing from the wall. There was a large metal pipe that ran low down the center of the room but as long as he was careful he didn't think it would be a problem.

It was perfect. He could stack the bricks, or at least most of them, back up. Nobody would notice it unless they were nosy anyway. And work was right next door. He knocked a few more bricks loose and shoved his trunk inside. He stacked the bricks until they covered about two-thirds of the opening. Satisfied, he headed off to another day at work.

Cindy was late to school that day. There wasn't another student or teacher to be seen. She was hoping she could grab her books from her locker and make it down to the AV room without anybody catching her. She closed her locker and turned around to see Principal Kane standing there shaking his head.

"Gosh, I'm sorry, sir," she said, "it wasn't my fault. There was this creepy looking guy and I had to take a different way and—"

"Ms. McNeil," Principal Kane said, "I couldn't care less about your tardiness. Your mother let us know about your disappearance. Frankly I'm surprised to see you back at all today. I'd actually like to have a word with you about a different matter."

Cindy relaxed. "Sure, sir. No problem. By the way, is that a new suit?"

"Where is Bronson Black?"

Cindy shrugged. "In class, I guess. What, am I his mother?"

"Ms. McNeil, both you and Bronson went missing two days ago. Not just any two days but the same two days. It doesn't take an investigative reporter to put two and two together. You two have hit it off and decided to skip together. There is a time and a place for young love, but—"

"Let me stop you right there. I haven't seen Bronson around for a couple days. I stayed at a friend's house for a couple of days. That's it."

"So you have no idea where Bronson is?"

"Oh. He's right there, sir," Cindy said as she pointed down the hall behind him. Principal Kane turned around. "Ya' big palooka," she whispered under her breath. Principal Kane turned back around.

"What was that?" he asked.

"Nothing, sir," Cindy said. "Glad we found him."

Bronson walked over. "Sorry I was out yesterday, Principal Kane. I was feeling pretty rotten and ended up falling asleep on the bus."

Principal Kane didn't look impressed with the excuse. "Well don't let it happen again, Mr. Black. Now both of you get to class."

Bronson sighed and started walking down the hall. Cindy joined him.

"You okay?" she asked.

"Not really. You see, my uncle kind of—"

"Oh, that's cute," she said as she skipped ahead of him. "You thought that I cared."

Bronson caught up with her and they walked along for a few minutes.

"So, how's that whole thing with the pollution going?" he asked.

"The mayor's office was weird. I did get to talk to the mayor before they kicked me out. I met this kid from the West Side though. He seems like he might have some good info for me. Nothing I can talk about until I get confirmation from the mayor's office but I figure I should probably lay low for a little before I barge in there again."

Bronson stopped and looked at Cindy. "Aw, they don't know an honest-to-God reporter when they see one," he said.

Cindy smiled at Bronson. He was pretty nice, for a twerp. Especially with how mean she was to him. But then she thought maybe he was making fun of her.

"Ya' know what?" she said, "I don't need a pep talk from a little squirt like you. See ya."

She turned down a hallway and left Bronson staring after her. He didn't know quite how to read her. Sometimes she was nice. Sometimes she stood up for him. Sometimes she picked on him. But overall she was the best friend he had right now. Well, except for Mr. Horum.

Later on in the magic shop Bronson stocked some shelves while Mr. Horum sat on his stool flipping through a catalog.

"Bronson," Mr. Horum said, "why you work here?"

"I needed a job and you were willing to give me one?" Bronson asked, a little unsure if it was the right answer. The old guy was taken to cryptic questions he already knew the answer to.

Mr. Horum walked over to Bronson and helped stock some tricks.

"What your job then?" he asked.

Bronson pulled three metal rings out of the box and tried to put them together. "I dunno. Helping and stuff," he said. He lost control of one of the rings and it clanged to the floor. Mr. Horum leaned over to pick it up, grunting as he did.

"Job is a—what you say? Trilogy? Trinity? Job is three parts." Mr. Horum took the other rings from Bronson and held one up. "First part is people. There are kinds of people. Clowns. Doctors. Bums even. They all important to us. We take care of them."

Bronson thought about his uncle. "But what if they're bad people?" he asked.

"Then we no let them do bad when they are here. But still we care. Show them tricks. Carry bags. We make them happy, hmmb?" Mr. Horum waved the second ring through the air. "Second part friendship. We work at same place. I'm your boss, but we still are friends. I show you new tricks; you show me some. We cover each other."

Mr. Horum leaned down and looked Bronson in the eyes. It seemed like he was looking for something, and then he found it and stood back up. "Right, second part no problem." He held up the last ring. "Third part respect. We no make excuse here. If you make mistake, you tell me and you learn. I teach you. You respect..." Mr. Horum linked the ring to the first one he'd held up. "Friends..." Mr. Horum linked the other ring to the third ring, "and job stay together. You no do this."

Mr. Horum shook the center ring and the other two other rings crashed at Bronson's feet. "The whole thing fall apart, you betcha." Mr. Horum handed Bronson the ring that was left. Bronson picked up the other two rings from the floor. He'd seen how Horum did the trick and copied it.

"Well then," Bronson said, "we'll keep them together."

The door opened and three boys around Bronson's age walked into the shop.

One of the boys walked over to Bronson.

"Ain't you the new kid at school?" he asked.

"Yeah, that's me," Bronson said.

"You work here?" another boy asked.

"Yeah," Bronson said.

"Pretty cool job. Well, see you around." The boys joined their friend to dig through the discount novelty bin. One of them pulled out a joy buzzer half-hanging out of a busted blister pack.

"I think this one's broke," the kid said.

Mr. Horum looked up from counting the day's deposit.

"Bring here please," Mr. Horum said.

The kid laid the joy buzzer in front of Mr. Horum. He picked it up and pulled it out of the packaging. He twisted it around a few times then pressed the button. It *BUZZED* in his hand.

"Hey, still work. You want? Only quarter."

"Nah, that's okay," the kids said. "We were actually leaving. Come on, guys."

The boys exited the shop. Mr. Horum turned the buzzer around in his hand for a moment.

"Hey, no need to waste toy. You want it?"

Bronson walked over and took the buzzer. He looked at it, pressed the button, and felt the buzz then shrugged.

"Sure," Bronson said. "Could you hand me my bag from back there on top of that box?"

Mr. Horum grunted as he leaned down and grabbed the bag. He handed it to Bronson. Bronson sat it on the floor and unzipped it. The first thing he saw when he opened it up was his Dogboy mask. He shoved the buzzer in the bag.

"You stealing that? I thought you seemed a little suspicious," said a female voice behind him.

Bronson turned around. Cindy stood behind him. She was holding a blond wig and a stage makeup kit.

"No. Of course not," Bronson said. "I work here. What's all that stuff for?"

Cindy grabbed a friction pen from a cup on the shelf next to her.

"Oh, nothing. Just doing some undercover work, you know. Reporter stuff."

Bronson threw his bag behind the counter then grabbed a plastic bag from a display on the front counter.

"Here, these might help." He handed her the bag. There were four foam earplugs in it. They were black and had a raised ring around the center.

"Just tear one in half and shove the one piece in each of your nostrils. It spreads out your nose. Makes your face look all different."

Cindy tucked the earplugs between the other purchases in her arms.

"Thanks, kid," she said. "Say, you have any of those glasses that make your eyes look all huge like an owl?"

"I think so. Let's look." Bronson led her to the far end of the store near the public restroom. There was a spinner rack filled with specialty spectacles. There were ones that lit up and ones with blacked out lenses and even a monocle or two.

Bronson picked up a pair with round lenses and handed them to Cindy.

"Here. These should do the—"

The bell at the front of the store rang, and a strange woman came through the door while she waved a gun in the air.

"Alright, you. Old freak behind the counter. Your gonna give me that money there."

Mr. Horum put his hands up in the air.

"You take it. Take whatever. I no care."

Bronson pulled Cindy down behind some shelves. He pointed to the bathroom door.

Cindy nodded and crawled toward the door. Bronson crawled in the other direction and moved toward the counter.

"I got this eye right here on you, friend," said the thief. "No funny stuff." She shoved the gun in front of Mr. Horum's face. Mr. Horum placed a stack of bills in a small bank bag then calmly used the free hand to push the gun away from his face.

"I do what you say, you betcha," Mr. Horum said. "Why be rude?"

Cindy made it through the bathroom door. The hinge creaked as it closed completely. Bronson jumped up with his hands raised.

"Don't shoot. I'm just hanging out back here," he said.

The thief gestured toward the counter.

"Get up here with the old man."

"Yes, ma'am." Bronson ran over to Mr. Horum's side.

"Let me ask you question while I give you

Horum's money," Mr. Horum said to the thief. "You know Horum. You know job at least. We should know you too."

"So what?" she asked. "You want my name?"

"You betcha. It help build trust, yeah?"

"Francine, and I'm gonna call you Mac and the kid Junior. Now let's fill up the bag, Mac."

Mr. Horum shoved the pile of bills into the bag. He zipped it up and handed it over to Francine. Francine unzipped it and flipped through the bills. A few fell out onto the floor and she leaned over to pick them up.

"What the blooming blazes is this?" she said. She held up Dogboy's mask. "Where did you get this?"

"You know this?" Mr. Horum asked Bronson.

"Never seen it before," Bronson said.

"Don't lie to a liar," Francine said. "This thing looks just like how old bucket head described that dog brat. Oh, old Francine is going to be eating steak with the boss man tonight, Mac. Now, seriously. Be completely serious. Some kid came in here and left this, right? Who's the kid, Mac? Junior over there?"

Bronson's ears buzzed and his breath became

something he had to concentrate on.

"I told you. I said I've never seen it," Bronson said.

Francine tossed the mask on the floor.

"Don't lie to a liar, Junior. We ain't leaving here until we figure it out." Francine backed up to the front door and locked it then gestured toward the back room with her gun. "Let's take this away from the window. Never know who's gonna walk by."

Mr. Horum and Bronson walked into the back room. Francine followed them and shut the door behind them. A moment later the bathroom door creaked open and Cindy crawled out. She peeked out from behind the shelves. Satisfied she was alone she stood up. She crept behind the counter and picked up the phone. She dialed 9-1-1 and after a few seconds there was a click on the line.

"911, please state your emergency," said an operator's voice.

"Robbery. Old Curiosity Shop on South 4th Street. She's still here. I gotta go." Cindy hung up the phone. *Hope they got that okay*, she thought. She certainly didn't want to be as close as she was to the gal with the gun so she decided to get outside and figure out if there was any way she could help Bronson and the old guy.

Cindy unlocked the door and opened it. The bell rang. She ran through it and raced down the street.

"What was that?" asked Francine.

"Somebody opened the front door," said Bronson. He was sitting on the floor underneath the window. His hands were tied with some fishing line Francine had found in the back. Mr. Horum was in a chair next to him with his hands and feet bound.

"Shoot. Guess I gotta go check it out. You fellas better start figuring out how that mask got in here while I'm gone. See this gun? It's kinda my buddy. We work real well together. If I'm gonna use it on ya' it's gonna do what I want. Got me?"

Bronson and Mr. Horum nodded. Francine opened the door and went out into the shop.

"Psst," came a voice from the window. Bronson looked up and saw Cindy dangling a small plastic bottle over his head.

"Get out of here, will ya?" Bronson said.

"You know this girl?" Mr. Horum asked.

"Yeah, she's a girl from school. She's the one who set off the bell."

"I also called the cops, thank you very much," Cindy said, "and I got this out of the makeup kit for you. It's astringent. It's not gonna kill her or anything but if you throw it in her eyes it'll burn like crazy." Cindy dropped the bottle and Bronson lifted his bound hands and caught it.

"Thanks," Bronson said, "now get out of here. No sense in you being in danger too. She'll be back any second."

"Aw, new kid, I didn't know you cared." Cindy disappeared from the window.

"You got girlfriend, boy-o?" Mr. Horum said.

"Yeah right," Bronson replied.

Francine walked back in and closed the door behind her. Bronson cupped his hands around the bottle.

"Door was open, nobody out there though. Almost like somebody was in here and snuck out when I was dealing with you two. Admit it. We're all friends here. We know each other's names. It was that dog brat, wasn't it?"

"Dog brat?" Mr. Horum said, "Horum don't know any dog brat. We no want any problems. Take money. Take stuff. Who care, right? We don't know about guy you looking for. Kids come in just before you get here but none of them dog. Just let us go and be safe now, hmmb? Store is yours. No problem."

Francine knelt down in front of Bronson. She laid the gun on the floor next to her and grabbed Bronson's collar.

"No. Mac don't know. But I bet Junior does. You got a taste for Alpo, little dude? See, I got this idea now that the mask just might'a been—Agh!"

The astringent hit Francine in the eyes. She grabbed her face and fell over on her side. Bronson kicked the gun across the room. He pressed his back against the wall and wiggled up onto his feet.

"Good boy," Mr. Horum said. "You get prize for that. Anything in store."

Bronson worked the fishing line against the corner of the window sill until it split. He shook it off his wrist. He ran over to Mr. Horum and got his limbs free.

"We should leave until the police come, right?" Bronson asked.

"You betcha," Mr. Horum said. "You okay, right?"

"You betcha, Mr. Horum. Let's go outside."

Mr. Horum stood up and opened the door for Bronson to walk though.

"Hold on," Bronson said, "I gotta grab my bag."

Bronson grabbed his bag from behind the counter then went around to the front and grabbed his mask. He shoved it in his bag then went out front to wait on the police.

10

Anchored and Sold on a Pillow of Stone

Hot John. Dogboy is captured.
Osbert. Blaze takes the blame.

It was midnight, and outside Colta City General Hospital it was quiet. Erica Torres, a nurse at the hospital, was lingering outside a side door and enjoying the night air. She was on her fifteen minute "smoke break," which is what she called it although she was one of the few nurses who didn't smoke. She figured if killing yourself slowly got you a fifteen minute break two times a shift then somebody who was making healthy choices deserved one too.

Across the street there was an agitated movement under a tree where the street light didn't reach. Erica felt a chill and decided it might be better to go ahead and cut her break short. She turned to head back in the side door and ran into a big block of a man. He looked like a prize fighter who'd lost one too many fights. Bald, muscular, and with a few important teeth missing. His left hand was gone, but in its place was a harness with a large wooden mallet attached to it. He gestured to the cigarette butts littered on the ground by her feet.

"Smoking is a real dirty thing," he said. "I ain't gonna let you work on sick people after smoking. It ain't... what's the word... like if it ain't clean?"

Erica didn't get the whole "mallet hand" thing, but she hoped he was just a concerned crazy and she'd be able to explain and get to the other side of the door. "I think the word you are looking for is sanitary," she said, "but I promise you I wasn't—"

"Yeah," he said, "it ain't stationary." He raised his mallet hand. Erica considered running around to the front of the hospital where the security guards could see her. She hoped there was somebody watching the security monitors in the station.

"No," she said. "Don't. Please!"

Blinding flashes of light popped all around her and the big brute. Sudden movement. A small person jumped between her and her attacker and hit him in the face. The sparks that were blinding her faded away and she saw what had to be a kid in some funky Halloween costume standing there while the bruiser rubbed his chin, looking more annoyed than anything.

"Get inside and call the police," the kid said in a nasally voice. "This looks like a job for Dogboy."

She was confused, but the kid had a point. She could be back there with guards in a minute. How much damage could the big guy do in that short of a time?

"Thanks, kid," she said as she ran back inside.

Dogboy backed against the door as it closed behind her. This guy was big alright. Bigger than any crook he'd faced in the past couple of weeks anyway. But he still looked a little dazed from the Wee Glimmers that Dogboy hoped would give him the advantage. The man cocked his head as his vision came back into focus.

"Dogboy?" he said. "Andrus was looking for a kid what dressed like a dog."

"Oh. Is there a reward? Because we can split the reward. I won't say a thing if you won't. One thing first, muscles—." Dogboy rolled under the man's legs and jumped up onto his back, digging his fingers into his eyes.

"I used to have a pup like you," the man said. "He was ornery." The man reached up and got hold of Dogboy's cape. "He used to play like he was fighting me too." He yanked Dogboy over his head and held him a couple of feet off the ground. The cape dug into his neck and he struggled to breathe. The man reeled back his added appendage ready to strike. "He don't play with no one no more."

Dogboy reached up to the clasp that held the cape on and released it. He dropped to the ground. He ran up and over a bench and leapt on top of a bus shelter. "Didn't your mom ever tell you it's not nice to hit people?" he asked, standing out of the big man's reach.

The man ran over and slammed the shelter with

his mallet. It shook and Dogboy lost his balance. He fell hard on the sidewalk and the man scooped him up and squeezed him tight in a bear hug.

"When you're as big as me you can do what you want," he said. Dogboy struggled against him. The man pushed Dogboy's face into his shoulder, pressing the plastic mask up against his mouth and stuffed up nose. Dogboy couldn't breathe, and the street lights turned into stars as the rest of the street faded away into darkness.

"Is it him?" Dogboy heard a voice ask as he came to. He decided to remain still until he could figure out what was going on. His eyes were hidden by the mask so he felt safe sneaking a peek. He was somewhere with a lot of trees and could hear running water off in the distance. Two men stood above him: the big guy from the hospital and Blaze from the parking garage.

"Yer darn tooting, Hot John," said Blaze.

"Hot John," the big guy from earlier, turned around. A portly man in a sweater vest and old-fashioned spectacles sat on a bench behind him, feeding some pigeons popcorn from a paper bag. "I done good, Osbert?" he asked.

"On the contrary, my brutish companion, you have done exceedingly well. I didn't expect one with such... meager aptitude to remember our leader's directive."

Hot John stood there like a dumb lump, unresponsive to anything he'd just heard.

"You 'done good,'" Osbert said.

"Wa-hoo!" Hot John said.

Blaze leaned down and plucked a blade of grass from the ground. He stuck it in his mouth and started chewing. Dogboy slipped his hand down toward the knife holstered on his ankle.

"Jonathan," Osbert said, "if you would be so kind as to transport our captive."

"Now hold up a darn second," Blaze said. "I deserve a crack at 'em I reckon."

"My dear friend," Osbert said, "remember: Andrus said the boy should be captured but that above all else he shouldn't be harmed. I know you want your revenge. Believe me, I want that for you. But it will come in due course. Besides, to do so would risk

Andrus's wrath. I think we can all agree that is the most unappealing option."

Blaze shuffled his feet. "I reckon yer' right. Guess I'll wait till some other night."

"Excellent," Osbert said. "Jonathan, if you could pick up the boy we'll be on our way back home."

Hot John stood there staring at Osbert as if he was a unicorn. Dogboy pulled the knife from his ankle and concealed it in his hand.

"Grab the kid," Osbert said. Hot John hoisted Dogboy over his shoulder. Blaze looked at him, remembering the night in the parking garage.

"I can't wait to tan yer hide, boy," Blaze said.

Dogboy lifted up his head and looked at Blaze.

"I double-dog dare you." He whipped the knife across Hot John's shoulder and landed on the ground. Hot John stumbled back holding the wound. Blaze lunged at Dogboy. A quick flash forward helped Dogboy dodge him and he ducked between Blaze and Hot John and ran as fast as he could. Osbert jumped in front of him but Dogboy slid between his legs.

Osbert plopped down on Dogboy's back and

caught his feet. His glasses fell off as he struggled to keep the boy from kicking him is the face.

"A rascally yea-forsooth knave," he grunted.

Dogboy couldn't move his body, but his arms were free. He reached back and tickled Osbert behind the knees. The fat man chortled and instinctively jumped away from the source of his merriment. Dogboy got to his feet and ran into the woods, disappearing from view.

Osbert picked up his glasses and walked over to Hot John and Blaze.

"A query," he said, "to what end can a brain function if the limbs do not cooperate?"

"You're confusing me again," Hot John said.

"I know, Jonathan," Osbert said. "I know."

Osbert went to the tree line and looked for any sign of the child. It was no use. He was gone, and Andrus would not be pleased.

From the Forward of the Unpublished Autobiography of Professor Osbert Collingwood:

I am an educated man. I received my undergraduate degree at Haverford and my graduate degree at Cambridge. I am (or was) a professor of business psychology but my real passion is classic British literature. Some people enjoy dancing or board games, but all I need to have a good time is a notepad and a Dickens text. Considering this, one might wonder how I found myself as one of the elite in a Guild of Thieves. It is a long, complicated story that takes up the lion's share of this book. If I had to point to one thing that aided my transition from high academic to low-brow delinquent it would be the heart and mind of our leader Andrus.

You might wonder how a man whose face I've never even seen could sway me to move from a university-provided apartment to an abandoned subway car underneath Colta City. It's a good question, and one I find myself asking on occasion. The academic life is rewarding philosophically if not financially. For one such as myself it lacked a social element, but there was a small pub I frequented on the weekends. One evening I arrived to see a cloaked man sitting in a darkened corner. The man was

Andrus. He intrigued me, so I bought him a drink at the bar and we sat in his corner until the wee hours discussing Kant and Brecht and Dickens and all the great minds of every age.

We left the pub together as the sun peeked out over the buildings, and he asked me if I would come to a place where conversations like the one we'd just had happened every hour of every night... and the men having them did more than talk. They acted. He even offered to pay me. I accepted, and he took me back to the first version of his den of thieves. We were a dozen or so then, but we were passionate.

In this book, which I expect won't be found until years after I'm dead and gone, I will recount my adventures with Andrus. The triumphs, the failures, and how he took the dregs of our society and turned them into the ruling class. It was one of the best experiences of my life to be his right-hand man, his confidant, and I would say his most trusted adviser. Despite all of the power and trust he bestowed upon me, I have one regret about following my leader. I have never seen his true face. I would love to look into the eyes of the man who saved me and saw me for who I am. If it never happens, however, it has still been an honor.

Osbert, Hot John, and Blaze sat alone in Andrus's office waiting for him to arrive. They'd left instructions for the tunnel guards to have him come to his office as soon as he got there. Osbert turned to his two cohorts.

"Gentlemen," Osbert said, "I must implore you to let me inform Andrus of our failure. If all of us expect to leave this room with everything intact it is imperative we break it to him gently."

Hot John and Blaze nodded their heads in agreement. The door opened and Andrus stepped through and walked over to his chair.

"My three most trusted men requesting my presence? I'm expecting something earth shattering, but I'm not expecting anything good. What is it?"

Osbert wiped his palms on his corduroy pants and cleared his throat.

"Andrus, sir, tonight we had an encounter with the child you've taken an interest in."

"Dogboy?" Andrus asked. "Wonderful. Where is

the little scamp? I have questions for him."

"Well, sir, we weren't able to bring him in. You see—"

Andrus stood up and twirled his cane around in his hand.

"So you just caught a glimpse of him, then? Well then why go to all this trouble to meet with me? This could have been communicated in your nightly reports. You are wasting my time."

"Well, funny thing," Osbert said with a crack in his voice, "we had a hold of him for a few minutes thanks to Jonathan's excellent fighting skills."

Andrus walked over and pressed the cane into Osbert's chest.

"So you are telling me he got away?"

"Yes, sir," Osbert coughed out.

"That is utterly and completely unacceptable," Andrus said. "Details. Now. Everything. I want to know who I need to punish."

Andrus turned away from them disgusted. Osbert straightened out his clothes. "The boy interfered with Jonathan while he was out collecting," he said, "Jonathan subdued the boy—"

"I smashed him good, Andrus," Hot John said.

Osbert glared at Hot John and continued.

"After knocking the boy out, Jonathan brought him to our rendezvous spot near the outer edge of Dixon Park. The boy was unconscious as far as we knew. Blaze asked to assault the boy as a means of revenge for their previous encounter. As I was convincing him to give up such goals and bring him back here as instructed, the boy awoke, and despite my and Jonathan's best efforts to stop him, he escaped into the woods."

"And how did he manage to escape from three full-grown men?" Andrus asked. "Men who have all been trained to stop people no less? You're all professional thieves."

"Well, as you can see, he cut Jonathan with a knife, and he... this is quite embarrassing... he tickled me while I held him down."

"And you?" Andrus asked Blaze.

"He ran right past me, I reckon," Blaze replied.

Andrus returned to his chair and tapped his cane against the floor. He sat there for several minutes, and none of the other men dared say a word.

Whatever punishment he was concocting would be far more severe if they spoke out of turn.

Andrus picked up his cane and paced in front of them.

"I would be lying if I said I was pleased. However, your encounter with the boy has afforded us some insight into his ability, which I'll need a full report on as soon as possible. Nevertheless, mistakes were made."

Andrus stopped in front of Blaze and took his hat off of his head.

"Ego proceeded instruction, and inaction on somebody's part allowed this Dogboy to escape. Please, kneel on the floor, brother."

Blaze, shaking and scared, stood up and knelt on the floor in front of Andrus. Andrus tossed Blaze's hat down and took up his cane. He pulled on the end of the cane and it came lose, revealing a sharp blade.

"You are one of my most trusted men, and it breaks my heart to do this, but you have allowed this whelp to escape not once but twice. You are hereby relieved of your position and will be made an example of."

Andrus gestured to the door with his cane.

"Osbert. Hot John. You can leave now."

Osbert and Hot John left without any words of comfort to Blaze. They wouldn't even look him in the eye. The three men had worked together for months but with a few words from Andrus, Blaze became a stranger. Osbert closed the door behind him. As they walked down the hall Blaze's screams echoed through the dark hallway. By the time they reached the end of the hallway the screams had stopped, and they both knew they would never see Blaze again.

11

A Day Out at Dixon Park

Bronson replaces his cape. Skate Day in the park.
Bugs gets what's coming to him. Dogboy saves the day.

Mr. Horum slid his key into the cash register and the drawer popped open. He reached in and pulled out three crisp twenty dollar bills then handed them to Bronson. Bronson instinctively counted the money.

"No worry," Mr. Horum said, "is all there.

"And then some," Bronson said.

"You work good, you get raise. What the big surprise?" Mr. Horum winked at Bronson as he closed the register.

"Mr. Horum," Bronson said, "silly question. Do I get an employee discount?"

Mr. Horum arched his eyebrow. "What you want?"

"I need a cape," Bronson said.

Mr. Horum laughed at the boy. "What you need cape for? To jump buildings in single bound I betcha."

"I wish," Bronson replied. "No. To distract my audience. I do a little razzly-dazzly stuff with the cape and they won't be paying attention to what I'm doing with my hands." Bronson had to replace the cape that had been stolen from him the night before, but he wasn't sure Mr. Horum would be that accommodating if he knew his number one employee was moonlighting as a superhero.

"Why you need a cape to do tricks for friends, hmmb?" Mr. Horum asked. "Kids make fun of you if you wear big fancy cape."

"Um, there's this talent show. At school so it's like a real performance." Bronson hated lying to Mr. Horum, but he couldn't bring himself to be honest with him either.

"Enough said. I got the best cape for you, I betcha." Mr. Horum ran in the back room and returned a moment later with a roll of a black velvet material. He whipped the roll out and Bronson saw it was a fine cape with a high collar. A real magician's cape. It almost looked like it could belong to a wizard. "This cape I wear when I do magic for shows. You like?"

Bronson touched the fabric. Smooth. He noticed a little pocket inside the cape. That could come in handy for some of his tricks. He picked the cape up off the counter and put it on. He flapped out the sides of it and felt as it waved through the air. Yes, this would do just fine.

"It's great, Mr. Horum," Bronson said. "How much?"

Mr. Horum frowned at Bronson. "We friends, right?"

"Sure," Bronson said.

Mr. Horum scratched his head. "And what friends do again?"

"Cover each other?" Bronson asked.

"Ah-ha. And what cape do?"

"It covers me," Bronson replied.

Mr. Horum clapped and danced around. "Smart boy. No charge. I cover you. You cover me. We cover each other."

Bronson didn't know how to respond to the gesture. People usually didn't just offer him things.

"I... thank you," Bronson said. "You know, Mr. Horum, I think you might be my best friend."

Mr. Horum ruffled Bronson's hair as he took the cape off. "Sad for boy like you to have old Mr. Horum as best friend. Now you go. You hard worker, but you need to be kid, too. Make friends with kids, you know?"

"I'll try, Mr. Horum," Bronson said.

Dixon Park was known the world over as one of the premiere destinations for skateboarders, rollerbladers, and other urban athletes. Any skater worth his salt had spent time grinding the rails and park benches in the park. For awhile Colta City tried to distance itself from that image. They'd even tried to ban it at one point but a protest by a 90-year-old man who liked to see the park being used squashed that pretty fast. He'd hopped on a skateboard himself and tried to get the police to arrest him. The image of this elderly man rocking back and forth on a skateboard while two younger men supported him as he yelled at a couple beat cops to take him in was a powerful image. WRDB reporter Kathleen Hayworth was there that day with her camera crew to capture the iconic image. Today, however, she was more or less phoning it in.

She was in Dixon Park again, underneath a banner that read "WRDB TV 3 PRESENTS - SKATE DAY IN THE PARK." Kids zoomed around on skateboards. Others practiced parkour on the playground. Still others sat on the grass enjoying the food and drinks provided by the TV station.

Kathleen checked her teeth and hair in a small mirror then took a swig from her bottled water. Cindy, her student intern from a local middle school, positioned herself behind the camera and waved her fingers 5... 4... 3...

Kathleen snapped into character. "Thanks, Dave," she said through a pasted-on smile, "we're out here today for WRDB's big Skate Day in the Park.

Children from several schools have come together for a fun day of sun and skating, and it's all brought to you today by WRDB CARES. Join me at six for highlights from the day. This is Kathleen Hayworth, reporting from Dixon Park."

"Clear," Cindy said as she lowered the camera.

Kathleen set the microphone on the ground beside her. "Did I look okay?" she asked.

"You looked great. Very professional," Cindy said.

"That is exactly what I wanted to hear. You're good at this," Kathleen said. "Why don't you take the other camera out and grab some B-Roll. We'll meet back here in an hour for interviews."

Bronson was also at the park that day and was standing around watching the kids doing parkour on the playground. He recognized one of the kids from a few weeks ago that he'd met outside of his uncle's apartment. A few minutes later Bronson walked up to the kid as he was eying up a new path.

"Hey," the kid said, "how goes it?"

"Great," Bronson said. "How 'bout yourself?"

"Okay. Some crazy crap went down but I'm good

now."

"Good to hear," Bronson said. "I've been dealing with crazy crap times a thousand. But, hey, that stuff you showed me a couple weeks back... works pretty good."

"Tight. You got moves? Show me."

Bronson didn't think showing off with all of kids from his school around seemed like a great idea. "Aw, I can't right now," he said. "I had a little problem with my back a couple days ago." It wasn't a complete lie. Osbert falling on him wasn't pleasant.

"You don't got to play with me," the kid said. "You ain't practiced once, have you?"

"No, I have," Bronson said. "Anyway, I just wanted to thank you. Oh, I never got your name."

"Axle," the boy said as he extended his hand to Bronson. "My bros call me Axle."

"I'm Bronson," Bronson said as they shook hands. Bronson looked over Axle's shoulder and saw Cindy shooting some footage of the kids sitting on the grass. "Gotta go. Thanks again."

Bronson ran over and tapped Cindy on the shoulder.

"Hey, I'm filming here," Cindy said without looking at him. He stepped several feet away and waited for her to finish.

Cindy took the camera off her shoulder and turned around. "Oh, it's you. Sorry, I'm shooting stuff for WRDB. It's pretty important."

"That's great," Bronson said. Cindy was surprised rubbing it in was kind of anticlimactic, but Bronson was happy for her. "You got a couple minutes?" Bronson asked. "I'll grab us some hot dogs."

Cindy's first instinct was to say no, but a hot dog did sound pretty good. "Sure, kid. I'll be over there," she said as she pointed at a bench.

Bronson came back a few minutes later with two hot dogs. He held out one to Cindy just as Bugs rode by on his skateboard and snatched it out of his hand.

"Thanks, miss. I'm starving," Bugs said.

Bronson grabbed the back of Bugs's shirt and he fell off the skateboard. Bronson knew it wasn't a good idea, but he was getting real tired of this kid. He wondered how Bugs would react if he knew he was picking on a superhero.

"That's for Cindy, jerk," Bronson said.

Bugs jumped up and pushed Bronson back. "You just messed with the wrong guy. I'll take both you and your little girlfriend down." Bronson wanted to hit him. He wanted to change into Dogboy and show Bugs who he was really messing with.

"That's fine, Bugs," he said. "Sorry. Just take the food and go."

"That's what I thought," Bugs said. "Thanks for the food." Bugs took a bite of the hot dog and skated off.

Bronson walked over and sat down next to Cindy. She still seemed pretty mad. He looked down at the hot dog he had left and figured he'd do the right thing (although he hated to give away free food).

"Here, Cindy," he said as he handed her the hot dog. She didn't look at him, but she took the hot dog and inhaled it. "If there weren't all these people around I swear I would have clobbered that guy."

Cindy stood up, took a few deeps breaths, and turned to Bronson. "Butt out, new kid. I don't need you sticking up for me. I'm not afraid of him or the teachers or anybody." Cindy stood up and shoved the camera in Bronson's lap. "I'm gonna kick his butt." Cindy ran after Bugs.

"Cindy," Bronson called after her. His vision went orange and he saw Bugs knocked out near the statue of Cassandra stealing the Eye of Apollo that was near the fountain in Dixon Park. He came back to the present and ran after Cindy, hoping he could stop her for both her and Bugs's sake.

Osbert waddled down Sansom Street near the entrance to Dixon Park. Hot John walked behind him with a bandage on his shoulder. He squinted against the sunlight. It was against Guild protocol to wander around during daylight hours, but for some reason Andrus thought that Dogboy would be there that day. Osbert suspected that Andrus was setting them up, but he didn't think Andrus a fool and hoped that he wouldn't have his two most trusted members arrested.

"There's sure a lot of cops, Osbert," Hot John said. Two policemen stood at the gates to the park, and there was a dozen or more inside.

"Andrus knew there would be," Osbert replied.

"Kids ain't clean, though. Most of them are big snotballs," Hot John said.

Osbert pulled a pack of moist towelettes from his vest pocket. "Fear not, my obsessive-compulsive compatriot. These claim to kill 99.9% of germs." Hot John reached for the towelettes and Osbert pulled them away. "Ah-ah, Jonathan," Osbert said, "not until after we're done. Or do you want to share in the same fate as our cowpoke friend?"

"That ain't funny," Hot John said. "Andrus ain't—
"

"Andrus *isn't* going to harm us as long as we get the boy," Osbert said. With that they walked into Dixon Park.

Cindy chased Bugs through the crowd. She knocked some sixth graders over, and she's spilled some guy's drink, but she was keeping up with him. In the distance was the statue. Bronson picked up speed and touched her shoulder. Normally a person would take that as a cue to stop, but Cindy was so intent on taking Bugs down she didn't even notice the additional resistance. She kept running but

Bronson's hand held her back. Her feet flew out from under her and she landed flat on her butt.

"You should start running now," she said while she winced.

"Cindy," Bronson said, "don't fight Bugs. We both know you would win. What's the point? What if you hurt him real bad?"

Cindy got back up and smacked Bronson's temple. "He's a bully," she said, "and nobody ever pushes him around. I'd pay to see that. Kid deserves it."

"Somebody get this creep offa me," Bugs shouted from over by the statue. Hot John was holding Bugs over his head while Osbert stood beside them pawing his vest. *Not them. Not here.*

Cindy snatched her camera from Bronson and started filming. "This is going to be good," she said.

Bronson needed to deal with these crooks, and he figured here was as good a place as any. Lots of cops around so hopefully they'd get arrested.

"Nuts," he said to Cindy, "I'm... uh... late for work."

"Fine. Miss all the..." She turned her head to look at Bronson, but he was gone.

"Fun?"

Kathleen ran up and jumped in front of the camera. She was carrying her microphone and shoved the cable at Cindy's face.

"Start shooting," she said. "This is actual news."

A few policemen surrounded the two criminals. One of the officers put his hand on his gun. Hot John put Bugs in a big bear hug. Osbert held up his hands.

"Officers," Osbert said, "as Oscar Wilde once wrote: 'Do not rise. It will avail thee nothing.'" He pulled his vest up and showed off a patched-together bomb with a digital timer mounted on the front. The policemen all took a couple of steps back.

A dozen yards away from the statue two storm grates popped open. Dozens of thieves slipped out and into the crowd. They approached the policemen from behind and overtook them, forcing them to the ground.

"Thank you, officers," Osbert said.

Bugs fought hard against Hot John. But every wiggle caused him to hold Bugs tighter.

Osbert put his vest down and adjusted his glasses. "My conscience would suffer if the boy was to come to harm, but the man who holds him now doesn't suffer from that scruple." Hot John grabbed Bugs's arm and twisted it just hard enough to get him to cry out without hurting him.

"We're looking for a boy that dresses like a dog," Osbert said.

Dogboy jumped out from the crowd. He'd stayed back to get a read on things but why not give the people what they want?

"Hey, cranky," Dogboy said, "long time, no eat?"

"This would be him," Osbert said.

Dogboy took a step toward them. "Let him go," he said.

Osbert walked over to Dogboy and knelt down to look him in the eye slits.

"We'll trade him," Osbert said. He pointed at Dogboy. "One boy for another."

Dogboy pulled his knife out of the pocket on his new cape and approached Osbert. Several members of the crowd shouted at him to stop.

"Listen to them, Dogboy," Osbert said. "Don't be

the fool who fights when he's already been beaten."

"There's not many other ways to deal with bullies like you," Dogboy said.

Kathleen leaned over to Cindy. "D'you get that?" she asked.

"Oh, I got it," Cindy replied.

Dogboy took another step toward Osbert. Osbert waved his hand in the air. "Proceed, Jonathan," he said.

Hot John pulled back his mallet hand and cracked Bugs in the nose. Bugs screamed as blood started dripping down his lips. Cindy smiled behind the camera.

"So," Osbert said, "will you come with us, or do I allow my brother here to have his fun?"

Dogboy felt a little satisfied when he saw Bugs get what was coming to him, but he knew if he didn't save him Hot John might kill him. He placed the knife back in his cape and held up his hands. "Fine," he said, "I'll come with you. Just don't hurt anybody."

Hot John lowered Bugs to the ground while the scattered thieves formed a circle around him, Osbert, and Dogboy. They moved to an open sewer grate across the way. Osbert flashed the bomb under his vest to the police as they passed.

They arrived at the grate. Hot John jumped down first. He held his hand up to Dogboy to help him down. Dogboy brushed it aside and jumped down past him. Osbert sat on the edge of the opening. "Don't follow us," he said to the crowd, "lest I explode this device. With that, my men and I shall humbly retreat."

Osbert jump down, followed by several of the thieves. Up from the hole flew the Osbert's bomb (no longer attached to Osbert). One of the thieves strapped it on. Everybody else went down into the sewers and the remaining thief lowered the grate and stood on top of it. He'd been instructed to stand there until the police apprehended him. That would give them all the time they needed to follow the sewers to the subway system, and from there they were home free.

Kathleen stood in front of Cindy's camera with her microphone. Cindy counted down with her fingers: 3... 2... 1...

"This is Kathleen Hayworth for WRDB Action

News, where the scene has turned tragic out here in Dixon Park. A WRDB Cares charity event was disrupted by a dozen men emerging from the sewers. They allegedly assaulted a middle-school student whose identity remains unknown at this time.

"His name was Bugs," Cindy offered from behind the camera.

Kathleen covered the mic and mouthed "I know" to Cindy. She continued. "The men also threatened the crowd with a crude bomb and abducted a small boy in a mask who was referred to as Dogboy throughout the altercation. WRDB was here on the scene and we'll be bringing the startling footage at 5 pm. Back to you, Dave."

The policemen grabbed the remaining thief and handcuffed him as they read him his rights. Cindy lowered the camera and ejected the memory cart so it could be captured in the news van on the way back to the station.

"So who do you think that Dogboy kid was?" Cindy asked Kathleen.

"I don't know," Kathleen replied as they sprinted across the park, "but whoever he was, he's probably dead now."

BILL MEEKS

12

In the Den of Thieves

Dogboy meets Andrus. Talking with Sister Francine.
The flood. Welcome to the Guild of Thieves.

Bronson couldn't see a darn thing. Once they'd
arrived down in the sewers they'd walked in silence
for a few minutes before coming to a door marked
SERVICE TUNNEL. Once through the door Hot
John had ripped his mask off and placed a black bag
over his head. They'd tied his hands in front of him
and Hot John slung him up over his shoulder. They
moved through the service tunnel into what sounded
like a big open space. They tied him to a chair and he

sat there in silence for several minutes until the faint sound of a shuffle-scrape came into the room.

"Ah, there he is," a voice said, "the famous Dogboy." The black bag was pulled off Bronson's head and he saw a man in a black hood standing over him.

"Why don't you take off that hood? You took my mask," Bronson said. "It's only fair."

The man—Andrus—laughed.

"Do you think life is fair, Bronson?" Andrus asked.

Bronson was startled. "You know my name," he said.

"Trust me," Andrus said, "you are important. You matter. I'd be a fool if I didn't study up on the infamous Dogboy. Humanity has been diverted onto a darker path. Stand with us and help arrest this regression."

"What the heck are you talking about? I don't even know you, mister," Bronson said.

Andrus leaned down and put his hand on Bronson's shoulder. "But I know you. A child. Lost. Alone. Hopeful that somebody will notice you long enough to realize that for all the confidence and bravado you are scared. You need a mentor...a guide. And anybody who could be that for you has cast you aside. Or left you. I know you, Bronson, because I've been where you are."

Bronson turned his head away from Andrus. "I don't need anybody. I'm doing just fine all on my own."

"Ah," said Andrus, "but who'll care that you're missing now? Will anybody notice when you don't go home? Will anybody notice if you don't make it to school tomorrow?"

Bronson turned and spit in Andrus's face. He was mad, mostly because Andrus was right. He didn't want him to be right, but he was.

"You don't know about my life," Bronson said.

"I was abandoned once. Cast aside in favor of somebody stronger. Then I found my brothers here in the guild. Now I don't have to be alone and neither do you."

A tear rolled down Bronson's cheek.

"You can still stand strong alone, sir," Bronson said.

"But haven't we tried?" Andrus asked. "And haven't we failed in spite of the trying? Nobody should have to go through this life alone, Bronson. Least of all a boy like you. With your gifts. You are needed. You—young, intelligent, powerful—you can help us." Andrus leaned in and gave Bronson a hug. "We can be each other's family, Bronson. You have a home here if you want it. We can teach you."

Bronson leaned into Andrus's shoulder and cried. About his parents. About Uncle Randolph. About Cindy and Bugs and living in an alley.

"There, there," Andrus said. "Don't worry, Bronson. Not anymore."

"But you're a crook," Bronson said. "I can't let a crook be my family."

"Things aren't as black and white as all that," Andrus said. "Come. I'll show you."

Dozens of thieves sprawled across the floor of the main meeting room. Andrus pushed a path through them. Dogboy followed close behind. They came to the back of the room where an old thermal blanket hung on the wall. Andrus pulled it back and led

Dogboy into a smaller room.

Sister Francine slept in the corner on top of a pile of dusty sleeping bags. A slew of clutter sat next to her: Old fast food wrappers, a few magazines, markers, and coloring books. Andrus shook her awake.

"Wait a second," Dogboy said. "She robbed my friend's shop a few days ago."

"Ay, it's Junior," Francine said. "I knew it was you. Big hero, throwing acid in my eyes like ya' did."

"I don't think I want to talk to her," Dogboy said to Andrus.

"Hold on," Andrus said. "Let her speak." He leaned down and patted Sister Francine on the shoulder. "Don't be afraid, sister." He looked behind her back. "Don't you be afraid either, son. Did you ever want to meet a real-life superhero?"

A little boy peeked out from behind her. He waved at Dogboy. Dogboy waved back.

"There are other kids here?" Dogboy asked.

"Of course," Andrus said. "Children are very important to the cause. None quite as important as you, of course, but we have several and we treat them quite well. Liam here already helps us on the street. Don't you, Liam?"

"Uh-huh," the boy said.

"How old are you, Liam?" asked Dogboy.

Liam looked at his mom. Sister Francine nodded.

"I'm 5... I think," Liam answered.

"Francine, tell the boy how you and Liam joined us," Andrus said.

"He's the enemy, ain't he?" Francine asked.

"Not anymore," he replied. "Dogboy is family now. Go ahead."

"Andrus has provided for us in so many ways. When we had to leave, after he... after my husband hurt our other son... Andrus found us. I was in a world I knew nothing about. The pain of remembering what he did was too much. I didn't want to remember. I would surely end my life if I thought about it too much. I left family, my friends, my home, my garden, and my dog. Chasing a means of survival that's not even real... money. Everybody out there judged who was important and who is not by how much we got or don't got. These folks took us in. They've taught me so much. Taught me how to survive. I'd be nothing and nowhere if it wasn't for this man. Liam and me... we owe him our lives."

"Isn't there anywhere else you could go?" Dogboy asked. "A den of thieves doesn't seem like the safest place to grow up."

"First of all we are thieves but we have honor," Francine said. "We are not criminals. We are freedom fighters. You'll see."

"He will, sister," Andrus said. "Thank you. And thank you, Liam. Sleep well."

Andrus walked Dogboy down to the drainage pipe that spat out at the south wall of the cavern. A few people sat in a circle around an old man. The man played an acoustic guitar and sang Spanish lyrics. An old bent woman spoke the words in English to the group:

Black storms shake the sky
Dark clouds blind us
Although pain and death await us
Duty calls us against the enemy

The most precious good is freedom

And we have to defend it

With faith and courage

Raise the revolutionary flag

Which carries the people to emancipation

Raise the revolutionary flag

Which carries the people to emancipation

Working people march onwards to the battle

We have to smash the reaction

"So what do you think?" Andrus asked.

"Everybody seems so... normal," Dogboy said. "If I didn't know where I was I'd think they were just regular people."

"They... we are regular people, Bronson," Andrus said.

"I know, but you're also crooks, right?"

"Sit down," Andrus said. Dogboy did as he was told. "Bronson, society has told these people every day of their lives that those lives are worthless. All because they didn't have the same chances others did. Money is the root of all evil and that is no lie. It gives some people confidence that was already inside them and turns some to a life of crime because of feelings of inadequacy. That is not this, Bronson. We do not feel inadequate. We are better than they think we are. When we are all equal and fully capable of supporting each other without money being the status by which we are all measured we can finally rest."

"But why do you have to steal from people?" Dogboy asked.

"By taking from them we teach them that money isn't important. When Independence Day arrives they'll understand that—"

White noise overtook Andrus's voice. The old man with the guitar jumped up.

"Everybody up," the old man yelled. "It's happening again!"

Water trickled out of the drainage pipe in the wall. Andrus grabbed Dogboy's hand and ran.

"Quick," Andrus said, "to higher ground."

The crowd in the cavern panicked. People ran into each other and over each other as everybody climbed up on anything they could.

"What's happening?" Dogboy asked.

"Every few months they drain the waste from that big drug factory by the river," Andrus said. "Everything flushes out right through here."

"Well shouldn't we go make sure everybody knows? It's the middle of the night."

"Let's get somewhere safe then we can assess the situation," Andrus said.

Andrus lifted Dogboy up onto a concrete pillar then climbed up himself. The noise became deafening. A thick pink frothy liquid like a strawberry ice cream float left in the sun too long poured from every pipe in the place.

"We have to go see if anybody needs help," Dogboy said.

"This stuff killed people last time, Bronson. I'm not going to let you go in there," Andrus said.

The levels continued to rise. The chemical runoff licked at their feet. It surged up over the edge and knocked Dogboy's feet out from under him. His head went under. The force of the water turned his mask sideways so he couldn't see. He ripped it off then looked around for something to grab onto.

He felt something pull at his feet. His head

snapped back as he got pulled into an undercurrent. He pumped his arms and legs as hard as he could but couldn't escape it. His lungs demanded air. He let go of his mask. It faded into the pink swirl around him. Darkness.

Light blinded Bronson as he came to on a ledge above the cavern. Andrus faced away from Bronson as he looked out over the chaos. He held his hood at his side.

"What's going on?" Bronson asked. Andrus pulled his hood back over his head then turned around.

"We almost lost you," Andrus said. "You're lucky I know basic CPR."

"You saved me?" Bronson asked.

"Of course," Andrus replied. He leaned back against the wall.

"Thanks," Bronson said.

"Help us! Help us!" came a voice from down below. Bronson looked down over the edge of ledge. The voice belonged to Sister Francine. A big clump of branches and leaves that the pink sludge must have dislodged pinned her against the wall below. She curled her arms around her son to protect him.

"Quickly," Andrus said to Bronson, "lean over the ledge. I'll hold your ankles."

Without a moment of hesitation Bronson leaned his torso over the edge of the ledge. Andrus grabbed Bronson's ankles then lowered him down. Bronson held out his hands to the trapped pair.

"One at a time. Hurry. Grab on and we'll pull you up," he said.

Francine gave her son a hug and a kiss on the forehead, then she offered him up to Bronson.

"Go on, honey," she said, "take his hand. It's a superhero here to save you."

The boy grabbed Bronson's hand. Andrus pulled them both back over the ledge.

"Ok, ready for one more round?" asked Andrus.

Bronson nodded. He went down over the ledge one more time. Francine reached out with both her hands and grabbed Bronson's. Andrus yanked on Bronson's ankles. Andrus couldn't move him. He teetered on the edge as he tried to get his balance back.

"I'm stuck on something," Sister Francine yelled

as the water began to rise again.

Bronson let go of her hands. "Get loose," he screamed.

The water rose even quicker. Sister Francine shook her head at Bronson as he felt himself being lifted up. As he made it back onto the ledge the water went up above her head and she disappeared under the current.

"You gotta go get her," her little boy said to Bronson. "You're a superhero. It's your job."

Bronson hugged the little boy. "I'm sorry. She's gone. She's been under too long. I tried—"

"No, no, you can help," the little boy said before he broke down in tears. Bronson hugged him as the water rushed below them.

A few hours later the cavern was dry again. Bronson rested in Sister Francine's room with his new friend Liam. Liam was curled up on the bed asleep.

Andrus came into the room and knelt down beside them.

"How is he?" Andrus asked.

"Tired," Bronson said.

"Here, we found this," Andrus said. He handed Bronson his Dogboy mask. Bronson took the mask and sat it on the ground next to him.

"Thanks," Bronson said. "Look, I've been thinking about what you said. About being family. I... I've missed that. I think I want to stay... on two conditions."

"That's great, Bronson," Andrus said. "But what are the conditions?"

"One: This kid gets taken to an orphanage or something. He doesn't belong here, especially without his mom."

"Done," Andrus said.

"Two: I need to go back up above ground tomorrow to say goodbye to some friends and get the rest of my stuff. And I need to go alone."

"How do I know you won't just go to the police and never come back?" Andrus asked.

"If you're that worried about it just wait until I get back to get the kid to safety, okay?"

Andrus considered it for a moment then nodded his head. "Fine," he said, "but get some sleep while you can. When you get back your training begins. Welcome to the Guild of Thieves."

13

Embrace the Underground

Bronson says his goodbyes. Andrus teaches Bronson how to be a thief.

Dogboy helps rob a train. A dangerous upgrade.

Bronson opened the familiar door to Mr. Horum's store.

Mr. Horum was behind the counter eating a pastry from the deli down the street. "Ah," he said, "there is that friend of mine—*the liar*."

Bronson had told Mr. Horum more than a few lies. He just didn't know which one he'd been caught in. Maybe it was a misunderstanding. "What are you talking about, Mr. Horum? I didn't lie to you about nothing."

Mr. Horum walked over to the small TV/VCR combo behind the counter and hit play.

"Not just liar," Mr. Horum said, "but liar who forgets he lie."

Footage from Dogboy's outing in Dixon Park played on the TV monitor. *There were news cameras there?* Bronson thought. *Wait. Cindy. Darn it.*

"—things took a turn for the worse," Kathleen said over the footage, "when the two men demanded a boy dressed like a dog show himself." Dogboy emerged from the crowd. "Police are unsure whether this 'Dogboy,' as he was called by the terrorists holding the park hostage, was a victim or in on the whole thing. They've received several reports in recent weeks of a boy dressed in a similar manner assisting in muggings around Colta City. If you have information—"

Mr. Horum paused the tape. "Oh, Ms. TV Woman. I have information for you, you betcha. You think I no recognize cape I give you, magician's son? My cape you need for 'talent show?' Hmph."

Bronson hung his head, ashamed of being caught

in the lie although he felt justified in telling it.

"I'm sorry, sir," he said.

"We supposed to cover each other," Mr. Horum said as he shut off the TV and walked over to Bronson. "Must I be friends with a liar?" Bronson realized he had the perfect opportunity to walk away without having to feel like a jerk for doing it. Mr. Horum already seemed like he'd given up on Bronson, just like everybody else.

"You aren't my friend," Bronson said, "You're just some lonely old guy who doesn't have anybody else." The words stung Bronson as he said them. The way he sounded reminded him of his uncle. He had a good idea how they made Mr. Horum feel.

Bronson walked to the door and turned around, trying to hide any emotion that was bubbling up inside him.

"I won't be in again," Bronson said, "I need to spend some time with my family."

Bronson slammed the door behind him, leaving Mr. Horum shocked. Sure, he'd laid it on a little thick, but he was just trying to teach the boy a lesson. Every second Bronson was in the store with him meant the world to the old washed-up magician. Mr. Horum was afraid that he'd never see his friend again.

Bronson crouched down and entered his little cubby hole of a home for the last time. He unlocked his trunk and made sure everything was there. He went around and packed up the few things he'd managed to buy since he'd started staying there: a couple of blankets, some books, a coat. He crammed them into the trunk then realized that he couldn't fit everything. He decided to pull out some odds and ends from the trunk and leave them there. It might not hurt to have a second base of operations if he needed something while he was out with the Guild.

He dragged the trunk to the entrance and blew out the candle. He was proud he'd lasted this long in these conditions. Most boys his age wouldn't stand a chance out on their own this long. But he wasn't giving up, he thought to himself, he was trading up. The Guild was offering him something he'd been looking for since the night his parents died: a home.

The subways in Colta City turned from subway cars into proper trains once they got about five miles out from City Center. The subway platform Bronson and Andrus hid behind was at Norberth, an affluent suburb west of the city. They'd followed the tracks all the way there. Andrus had explained to Bronson that it was a good place to start his training because people were far less suspicious in the suburbs as a rule. Bronson was dressed in street clothes so he could blend in, but Andrus insisted on keeping his hood on. He'd be staying under the platform.

Dozens of commuters lined up on the platform waiting on their trains. Bronson watched them with Andrus trying to find somebody who wouldn't see him coming.

"There," Andrus said, "that one." He pointed to a man in a suit who was playing a game on his phone. Bronson waited for the train to pull out of the station and jumped up on the platform. He crept up behind the man and reached for his wallet. His vision went orange and he saw the man sitting at a dining room table across from his wife.

"That was everything?" she asked him.

"My whole paycheck," the man replied. The women stood up and walked away from him. She began to cry as she held her pregnant belly.

"What about him?" she asked.

"We'll figure something out, dear," the man said as he put his arms around his wife. "We have to."

The vision was gone, and Bronson shivered. His hand bumped against the man and the man flipped around.

"What do you think you're doing?" he asked.

"Oh. Hi, I… uh, nothing. Sorry," Bronson said. He backed away and ran off as the man checked to make sure his wallet was still there. It was.

Back under the platform Bronson was trying to explain himself to Andrus. "I couldn't. He didn't deserve it," Bronson said.

"How would you know that?" Andrus asked.

Bronson didn't know if he was ready to trust Andrus enough to let him in on his power yet.

"I… just know," he said.

Andrus turned away from Bronson, ashamed. "You deliberately disobeyed me. You don't trust me."

Bronson realized he was about to make the same mistake he'd made with Mr. Horum. He decided he needed to be straight with Andrus if this whole situation had any chance of working out.

"I saw his home," Bronson said, "he needs his money. Sometimes when I'm right in the middle of something I get these... pictures in my head. Like what would happen if I didn't step in to change it." Bronson waiting for any reaction from Andrus.

"You can see into the future?" Andrus asked.

"Yeah," Bronson said.

"And that's why you disobeyed?" Andrus asked.

Bronson nodded his head. He saw orange and flashed forward to Andrus jumping at him, which Andrus did when Bronson came to. Bronson jumped to one side and Andrus landed on the ground behind him. Bronson turned back around to face him, afraid he'd be attacked again, but Andrus laid on the ground laughing.

"Amazing," he said. Andrus got up and put his arm around Bronson. He led him into the train tunnel.

"So you believe me?" Bronson asked.

"Of course I do," Andrus said. "What's not to believe? And you can't imagine how much this will help the Guild. Let's go home, son."

Bronson cringed a little at the word, but he had to admit it was nice to have somebody call him that again.

Andrus and Bronson sat across from each other as Osbert made some marks on the wall with chalk.

"So if we consider time a straight line," Osbert said, "then we must assume our young friend's 'present' exists as a single point on that line." He drew a straight line and marked an X on top of it. "We'll call this point Dogboy Alpha. If somebody is in danger the Dogboy of the future," Osbert drew a circle farther down the line, "or Dogboy Beta, will send information about said event to Dogboy Alpha, allowing him to address the problem."

Osbert drew a dashed line traveling down the main line to the original Dogboy.

"Fascinating," Andrus said, "but how can we use it?"

"The boy can predict the future," Osbert said. "He

is a walking warning system. By utilizing this boy's talents we'll know about any potential danger before it happens. I predict an increased success rate."

"Find Hot John and take the boy out tonight," Andrus said. He walked over to Bronson and put his hands on his shoulders. Bronson felt a little spark of static electricity when Andrus touched him. It traveled down his shoulder and he felt his heart skip a beat.

"Go out tonight and try to get control over this power," Andrus said. "If you can control it we can use you. If not we do have contingencies."

Dogboy sat on a metal arch that hung over the subway tracks. Hot John and Osbert sat next to him. Neither had said a word in the hour they'd been sitting there.

"So," Dogboy said to Osbert, "any tips?"

Osbert smiled and leaned in closer to Dogboy. "Well, I suppose the most important thing is how to handle being apprehended by the police. In a word, play dumb. Never make eye contact. Never give an answer more than three words long. Don't react to what they say to you. Pretend to be bored. Either they'll give up on you and release you or give up on you and lock you up. Either way you win."

"Bored, got it," Bronson said. He turned to Hot John. "How about you? Andrus says you guys know a lot."

Hot John got a serious expression on his face. He looked out into the air in front of him. "Smash them before they smash you," he said. He got a smile on his face big enough that you could see every place he was missing a tooth.

Dogboy checked his new knife holster under his shirt. Andrus had given him a little money to upgrade some of his equipment and he figured it would be a lot easier to pull a knife off his back than off his ankle. The holster still felt a little weird to wear, but he was dying to try it out.

A train pulled up underneath them. Osbert pointed down. He held up his hand. The train's brakes squealed as it rolled to a stop. Osbert lowered his hand and the three of them jumped on top of the moving car. Osbert and Dogboy crouched down as the train entered the tunnel.

"Now what?" Dogboy asked. Osbert pointed toward the center of the car. Hot John was standing over a small hatch. He pulled on the metal door and it popped open. He looked down inside and seeing nothing there motioned for the rest of his crew to follow as he jumped down into the car. Dogboy and Osbert shuffled across the top of the car as it picked up speed. Osbert made it to the hatch well before Dogboy. He was steadier because of his "lower center of gravity." He jumped down onto Hot John's shoulders and held his hand out for the boy.

Dogboy was having trouble keeping his balance as the train went faster and lowered his body until he was crawling across the top. He reached out and grabbed Osbert's hand. Osbert pulled him over and down into the empty subway car.

"Thanks," Dogboy said, "I think I was about to—"

"Shh," Osbert sounded. He pointed toward the exit door at the front of the car. Osbert led them in a low crouch to the door. He peeked into the adjacent car and spied several passengers doing their best to not notice the others.

"Now," Osbert whispered, "try to use your gift.

Don't wait for it. Make it happen."

Dogboy sat down, closed his eyes, and concentrated. He squeezed his eyes shut so tight that all he could see for a little bit was a kaleidoscope blob of color. He concentrated harder, blocking out the sound around him as best he could. The blob faded to nothing. He breathed in and out and in and out and the nothing burned up in bright orange.

He was in the next car. Hot John slammed open the door and started yelling at people to give him their stuff. A man in a green suit pushes his way toward the front of the car. Dogboy and Osbert come through the door to help collect. The man gets within a few feet of Hot John and pulls out a gun. He tells them to freeze and—

The vision was gone. Dogboy opened his eyes. Hot John and Osbert were staring at him expectantly. Dogboy's head was throbbing like he had the most intense ice cream headache in the world. He shook his head around a little bit and the waves of pain began to subside.

"Well?" Osbert asked.

"It worked," Dogboy said, "wait for the man in the

green suit to get off." He leaned up against the wall of the car and tried to catch his breath. He reached up into his mask and pulled out the tissues he had stuffed up in his nose. What was the use of changing your voice when you didn't have a secret identity anymore? He pulled the right one out and noticed it has a few spots of blood on it. When he pulled the left one out he noticed it had a lot of blood on it. He reached up and touched under his nose. No more blood. Hopefully the tissues had been enough to stop the nose bleed.

The train rolled to a stop and a few passengers got off the adjacent car, including the cop in the green suit. The train started moving again. Hot John stood up and ran through the door with his mallet hand raised. A man near the door stepped in front of him. He picked the man up and threw him into some empty seats.

"Hey, listen," he said to the surprised passengers." We want what you got or else I pound all of you."

Osbert stepped through the door offering a bag to the people on the train. Dogboy was supposed to be with him, but Osbert had to leave him behind. He was back in the other car lying on the floor and shaking. Blood trickled out the edge of his mask.

Hot John and Osbert collected what they could and headed back to the empty car. Hot John looked down at Dogboy.

"This kid," Hot John said, "what a wuss." He handed Osbert the loot bag and picked Dogboy up. The train came to its next stop and the trio stepped off and made their way back to their den.

14

Trouble at Woodrow Wilcox

Bugs makes nice. Uncle / teacher conference.
Randolph makes a scene. Mayor Lane visits area schools.

Bronson was back in school for the first time in almost a week. It wasn't the classes that brought him back. It wasn't Cindy, who was sitting across from him at the lunch table scribbling in a notebook. It was the free food. The glorious microwaved pizza free food that he was shoving down his gullet.

Cindy sighed as she put down her pen. "Seems like the police should be able to find some stupid kid in a Halloween costume," she said. She looked around the lunchroom to make sure nobody was listening in. "Unless he has powers," she whispered across the table.

Bronson choked on his pizza and spit it into a napkin. "Yeah, right," he said. "What is this? A comic book?"

"No, for serious," Cindy said, "These kids from the West Side—"

"Maybe you shouldn't be digging," Bronson said. "He might wear that mask for a reason, you know."

"Like what?" Cindy asked.

"Maybe to protect the people he cares about? Or maybe just to cover his own butt."

"Hmm," Cindy said, "is that why you would do it? Wear a mask?"

"I wouldn't do what that kid's doing with or without a mask," Bronson said. "What kind of normal kid goes out at night to fight adults?"

"I don't think I'd wear a mask," Cindy said, "but I'd still try to keep it a secret, especially if I had secret powers. I'd pretend like I didn't have them and then when I needed them—BOOM- powers. But I'd never let anybody see me. I'd be a secret guardian angel kind of hero I think."

"You've put a lot of thought to it," Bronson said.

"Well, in a world where kids are running around fighting crime dressed like dogs I figure it pays to consider all the options."

Bugs walked up to the table on a pair of crutches. He also had a bandage across his nose. He nodded at Bronson then looked away. Under his breath he mumbled "I'm sorry about the other day."

"What?" Cindy said. "I don't believe it. Bugs? Apologizing?"

Bugs turned to Cindy. "I'm sorry for messing with you and the new kid, okay? I was a jerk."

Bronson couldn't take it anymore. He was just supposed to forgive him? After all the grief Bugs had given him since he arrived in Colta City he was just supposed to give up? Fat chance.

"Get away from us," Bronson said. He seized one of Bugs's crutches then shook it. "Or else."

Bugs put up his hands. "Okay, okay, sorry to bug you." He yanked his crutch away from Bronson and walked back over to his friends on the other side of the lunchroom. Bronson thought it was pretty funny.

Cindy kicked him in the shin under the table. It hurt.

"What was that for?" Bronson asked.

"He apologized, you jerk," Cindy replied.

"I thought you'd be impressed," Bronson said.

"Geez. Free pizza isn't worth this hassle. See ya." Bronson picked up his tray and turned around— then proceeded to spill his tray all over the front of Principal Kane.

"Bronson," Principal Kane said, unflinching with unfinished food dripping down his suit. "I need to see you in my office. Now."

Bronson slumped in the wicker chair that sat opposite Principal Kane. The principal was staring across his desk at Bronson, who did his best to not make eye contact.

"What's this about?" Bronson asked.

"Your teachers tell me you haven't been turning in your assignments," Principal Kane said, "and you haven't been in homeroom in over a week. Anything to say for yourself?"

"Excuse me," Bronson replied.

"And then I come up to you in the lunchroom and you're saying the school doesn't matter to you anymore. What's going on, Bronson?"

Bronson leaned back in the chair and folded his arms.

"Who needs school?" he said.

Principal Kane shook his head and hit a button on his phone.

"Send him in, Michelle," he said. "Bronson, I've asked your guardian to come in for a little conference."

The door swung open and Randolph walked in. Bronson dropped the cool guy act and turned to the principal. "No, not him. He threw—"

Randolph dashed over to Bronson and covered his mouth. "I threw a fit when I heard about this, Principal Kane, sir. I assure you we *will* make sure he studies. And attends school. Bronson was wrong, your highness. All is fixed. I'll handle it… God as my witness. You'll be good from now on, won't you, Bronson?"

Randolph lowered his hand to Bronson's shoulder and squeezed just hard enough to get his point across.

"Sure, yeah. I'll be good," Bronson said.

Principal Kane sat back in his chair. "Thank you, Mr. Black. If more parents were as direct and involved in their children's lives as you I'd be out of a job."

"If only," Randolph said with a sneer. He pulled Bronson up by his arm. "Come, Bronson."

"Well, Mr. Black, Bronson does have classes to attend," Principal Kane said.

"Oh, I just need to talk to him a moment. Then right back to class," Randolph said.

With that Randolph pulled Bronson out the door. Bronson was prepared for the worst. He wasn't going to let this guy push him around anymore.

Randolph pushed Bronson out the front doors of Woodrow Wilcox Junior High. Bronson recovered and spun around to face his uncle.

"Why are you here?" he asked.

"When a truant officer comes to my door in the middle of the day I tend to take an interest in the goings-on surrounding it," Randolph said. He pushed

Bronson up against a tree. "You will go to school. If I open my door to a cop again—well, you know how often little runaways pop up in the harbor."

Bronson spit in Randolph's face.

"You bold little—" Randolph smacked him. Bronson pulled back and swept Randolph's leg out from under him with a quick kick.

"I wouldn't expect any less from Duncan's son," Randolph said. "You've got a bit of your dad in you, but I'd be careful. If we weren't family—"

"I have a new family now," Bronson said. "They won't let you hurt me."

Randolph smiled at Bronson and let him go.

"Oh, I don't know," he said, "might not like them once you get to know them."

A town car tailed by two policemen on motorcycles pulled up in front of the school. Randolph jumped up and hugged Bronson tight.

"Don't miss school again," Randolph said into Bronson's ear, "but if you do you might as well just head straight back to that hovel you came from." Randolph patted Bronson on the head then walked down the street.

A man in a dark suit and sunglasses got out of the passenger's side door of the car. He looked at his clipboard, then at the school, then back at the clipboard, then back at the school.

"This is where she goes, sir," the man said back into the car.

The back door opened and Mayor Lane stepped out. Bronson waved.

"Hello there, young man," Mayor Lane said. "We're here to have a word with your principal. Could you point us in the right direction?"

Bronson pointed at the doors to the school.

"Through those doors, left, right, right, left. Can't miss it," Bronson said.

"It's right in here, sir," Principal Kane said as he led Mayor Lane and his assistant Chester into the AV room. Cindy sat at an ancient teleprompter typing in scripts for that afternoon's show.

"Ms. McNeil," Principal Kane said, "I'd like you to meet Mayor Lane. He's here to tour the school and wanted to see the newsroom. Think you could show him around and bring him back to my office when you're done?"

Cindy sat there staring at the men with her mouth hanging open.

"Ms. McNeil," Principal Kane said, "if you ever expect to make your career in journalism you can't be starstruck. Get over here and shake the mayor's hand."

Cindy put her stack of scripts down and walked over to the mayor. Mayor Lane smiled down at her and extended his hand.

"You seem very familiar, young lady," Mayor Lane said. Cindy couldn't tell if he messing with her or not. She took his hand and shook it.

"Cindy McNeil," she said, "pleasure to meet you, sir."

"Well, looks like you're in good hands," Principal Kane said, "I'll leave you to it."

Cindy wasn't sure what to do, so she took a deep breath and went into her rehearsed speech. "WWJH was founded in 1978 a scant four years after we opened our doors. Our state-of-the-art technology allows students to—"

"Ms. McNeil," Mayor Lane said, "you know I'm

not here for a tour."

Cindy ran toward the door to the studio. Chester grabbed her then put her down in the chair behind the anchor's desk.

"Don't worry, Ms. McNeil," Mayor Lane said. "Give us five minutes, and as long as things go well we'll walk out that door and you'll never have to talk to us again. Okay?"

Cindy didn't really think she had a choice in the matter so she nodded her head in agreement.

"Good," Mayor Lane said. He leaned over the anchor's desk and stared Cindy down. "When you visited City Hall you may have seen some things... experienced some things... altered some things... That's fine. You made it out fair and square and I'm certainly not in the business of abducting children myself in broad daylight. I am, however, in the business of providing for my dear Colta City. And protecting her from those who would try to tear her down. Protecting her from people like you, Ms McNeil."

Mayor Lane reached into his breast pocket, pulled out a pine green matchbook then tossed it on the desk in front of Cindy. Large gold letters spelled *Erin's Pub* on the cover in a curly decorative typeface.

"I take it you know this place?" Mayor Lane asked.

"That's where my mom works, you jerk," Cindy said.

Mayor Lane smiled at Cindy. "Oh, is it? That's nice. It's a great little place too. To think... I was only a councilman when my company bought that property all those years ago. Sadly it hasn't been very profitable lately. Isn't that right, Chester?"

"Right, sir," Chester said.

"You remember Chester, don't you, Cindy?" Mayor Lane asked. "You were so rude though. You didn't even say goodbye to him when you left. Not like you did to me anyway."

"What do you want, jerkwad?" Cindy asked.

Mayor Lane smiled as he put the matchbook back in his pocket.

"I don't want anything from you, Cindy. I want *nothing* from you. Go back to your life here. Make your news show, take your tests, forget about your visit to City Hall. Do that and I'll see to it that Erin's Pub stays open in perpetuity for as long as your mother works there."

Cindy held out her hand. "Deal," she said.

Mayor Lane shook his head. "Ah, ah. No need for that again. We'll just call it a deal and leave it at that, okay?"

"Sure," Cindy said. She was lying of course. Before this moment she'd planned to walk away from everything that happened. Now, though, she wasn't going to rest until Mayor Lane was Inmate Lane... and she knew just the kid to call to make that happen.

15

The Ghost in the Subway Car

Dogboy becomes an asset to the team. Andrus brags about him.
Bronson flies and falls. An old foe returns.

Paulus, Kathleen. "Guild of Thieves Baffle Police." Colta City Herald 24 Jun.

Police are still trying to piece together a mysterious spa heist that occurred on the twenty-seventh block of Oakland Street today. Missy's Nails 'N Things was robbed at gunpoint at 6 pm this evening by a group of several armed men. Most of the men wore masks. Witnesses claim a boy dressed in a dog costume was present, but police are unsure if it was the same boy seen in Dixon Park last week or a copycat. Police say the only clue they have to go on is a piece of paper found in an alleyway behind the spa that read "For Andrus."

Dogboy stood near the back door of the spa holding a couple gym bags stuffed with cash, purses, and jewelry. The items belonged to the ladies Hot John was tying up in the middle of the room. One of them reached out for Dogboy's arm.

"Honey, you seem like a nice boy," she said. "Why are you running around with these hoodlums? You shouldn't get caught up in such things."

"I'm fine, ma'am," Dogboy said. He turned to Hot John. "Do we have to tie them up?" he asked.

"Andrus's orders," Hot John said.

Esperenza, Carlos. "Dogboy: Villain or Victim?" Free Press 29 Jun.

A local shopkeep claims he was robbed by the infamous Dogboy, who went missing in Dixon Park during an attempted terrorist attack. There have been several reported sightings of Dogboy since his first appearance and subsequent disappearance. Gregory Prattle of the Oliver Street Stop and Save showed us pictures that appear to show Dogboy, accompanied by a large portly gentleman. In them, Dogboy attacks Prattle outside his shop. The boy threw small red flares into Prattle's eyes then took his wallet. Prattle was released from the hospital today with no serious injuries. An anonymous police representative said they believe the boy is being coerced based on his exchange in Dixon Park the day he disappeared and that witness accounts of the incident support that belief.

Osbert and Bronson sat in a subway car on the way back from a robbery. Bronson flipped his mask around in his hands while he thought about what he'd done.

"I hope the glimmers didn't blind him permanently or anything," Bronson said.

Osbert smiled at the child. "Don't you remember what Andrus told us this morning, my dear boy? The property owners, the businessmen, they are the real enemies in this war. War is hell, as they say, and there are bound to be casualties. But they shouldn't matter if you fight for the right side."

"But how do we know we're on the right side?" Bronson asked.

"We know when we win," Osbert said.

Delroy, Timothy. "Hammer-Handed Henchmen Hampers Health." The C.C. Inquirer 27 Jun.

Disaster struck in a local Kraftburn's Grocery Store on the West Side today. A large man allegedly used a giant mallet to assault several customers and employees today in a daring robbery attempt. Police say descriptions of the assailant match those of the bandit who assaulted a local middle-school boy earlier this month. The store is offering a $100 reward for information leading to the capture of the man, who left one bag boy in serious condition after *his rampage.*

Bronson sat across the street from Kraftburn's Grocery watching for the police. He saw Hot John hit the bag boy through the big window on the front of the store. The bag boy's head caught the corner of his register. Blood spurted out all over the checkered linoleum. Hot John ran out of the store, and Bronson headed back to the subway.

Andrus held a copy of The Colta City Herald above his head. The headline read SECURITY UPPED FOR BIG FOURTH OF JULY BASH. Andrus ripped the newspaper in half and addressed the gathered guild in the meeting hall.

"Look at them in their foolishness. Laugh at their pride and confidence. They think themselves protectors while they wage wars and build atomic bombs and try to make us believe it's for our own good. They say they represent justice, yet they call us criminals. But we are the freedom fighters. We exist without bias or class or judgment. We possess a great knowledge. A superior science. We are the revolution."

The hall erupted into applause.

Andrus stepped stage right then motioned with his hand to somebody offstage. "I'd like to introduce you to our newest brother. This child is the guild's secret weapon. He is more powerful than you can possibly imagine. He'll bring us our victory. He'll turn the whole world upside down. My brothers and sisters, I give you Dogboy."

The crowd cheered. Andrus held his arm out toward the stairs to welcome their new star. The crowd chanted "Dogboy! Dogboy! Dogboy!" as Andrus stood there and smiled.

"Where is the little twerp?" he whispered to one of his men.

Bronson, as it so happened, worked away in an adjacent subway tunnel. He'd stumbled across it a few days prior. An abandoned subway car sat in the center of the tunnel. Both of its left wheels were missing so it tilted back off the ground. A broken pipe stuck out of the wall, a steady stream of what looked to be clean water poured out. Bronson washed his clothes in a bucket filled with the stuff. He had his trunk positioned behind him with several fresh items draped over it drying. He figured he'd hang them up and check out the old subway car while they dried.

Bronson scrubbed a mustard stain out of his cape. His vision went orange but he there was no flash forward this time. He heard a humming that built and built until it split through his skull. He tasted metal on his tongue, then heard a whispered wind as a voice cut through the air.

"*Bronson,*" it said.

Bronson's eyes rolled back in his head. Blood poured down from his nostrils. His body itself glowed with the familiar orange aura. It felt like a warm hug. He opened his eyes to see his feet dangling below him a few feet off the ground.

"How are you doing that? Who are you?" he asked.

"*You know who I am,*" the voice whispered. "*You know at the heart of you, son.*"

Bronson jerked his head around in the air to find the source of the voice.

"Dad?" he said. "It can't be you. You... you died."

"*I live on in you.*"

The aura around Bronson burned brighter as he bobbed up and down, moving across the tunnel toward the old subway car. "Can I see you and Mom again?" he asked.

"*No,*" the voice said, "*even though we miss you we are both happy here. Son, you waste your legacy. You live with cowards and thieves then call them family.*"

"It's not like I have any real family left," Bronson said. "Uncle Randolph kicked me out."

"*There are others willing to help you. You didn't have to resort to this.*"

Images flashed through Bronson's head: Mr. Horum, Cindy, Principal Kane, all with friendly expressions and outreached hands. He knew they cared. That's why it made it easier for him to push them away...Easier than waiting for them to leave him behind anyway.

"They aren't villains, Dad," Bronson said. "Andrus takes care of me. Look, I know on the surface he seems like a rotten crook, but he has reasons for what he does. Good-sounding reasons when he explains them. He's a good guy underneath everything."

"Is he?" the voice asked as Bronson's body drifted down to the ground beside the subway car. The orange aura faded.

"Dad?" Bronson called out into the cavern. "Dad, where are you?"

A groan echoed around inside the subway car, then it began to shake. Bronson scuttled around the car until he got to the doorway. The metal doors lay on the ground beside it. He couldn't see what was inside, but after another groan he took a deep breath and stepped in to investigate. As his eyes adjusted to the darkness he made out the figure of a man in the back of the car. He hung there, hands tied to the bar running along the top.

Bronson took a few steps toward the figure. A low sound came from the back saying "Heh he. Heh he." Bronson moved toward the back, afraid the man might be in trouble. As he got close the man let out a shriek like a slow death. Bronson took some Wee Glimmers out of his pocket. He moved toward the man with his hand out to show him.

"I'm not going to hurt you with these," Bronson said. "I just need some light so I can help you, ok?"

The man moaned in agreement. Bronson threw the Wee Glimmers against the ground. Blaze, the cowboy, from the parking garage weeks before stared back at him. Dried blood flaked off of his cheeks. His eyes bulged from their sockets, staring desperately at Bronson.

"Ha-ah," Blaze said, "Huh uhuh ahuh."

A small, black, and foul nub poked out of Blaze's mouth. Bronson couldn't believe it. Had Andrus done this to him? Blaze pulled against his bonds as he grunted loud nothings at Bronson. He jerked against the ropes. A loud pop echoed through the car. Blaze went limp, his right arm all twisted. He moaned in pain. "Uhh. Awl eh, ug, ooh ah," he said.

Bronson couldn't stand to see him in pain. He untied the first of the knots. As it came loose a large shadow blocked out the light coming through the door. Hot John stood there. He shook his head and gestured at Bronson with his mallet hand.

"Andrus ain't gonna be happy about this," he said.

16

Escape from the Underground

Dogboy asks for clarification. Escape from the underground. Mr. Horum gets one last customer before he closes up shop.

Andrus stood in front of a large blueprint of a stage that was taped to his office wall. He was studying the blueprints for security holes they could take advantage of on Independence Day. Osbert stood behind him looking through some notes.

"Your test results have surpassed all of my expectations, sir," Osbert said. "Remarkable progress. To be honest you are so adept I have to ask if this is your first time with--"

"Years ago, but only for a short time. And there was no chemical intervention required," Andrus said. "You understand how important it is we keep this between us I hope."

"Don't worry about me, sir," Osbert said.

"Thank you for your discretion, brother," Andrus said. "You can go. I'm expecting someone shortly."

Osbert saluted Andrus then left. Andrus picked the cane up off his desk. He stood in the middle of the room, faced the door, and waited.

Hot John barged through the door carrying Bronson. The door slammed off the interior wall.

"I didn't ask you to manhandle the boy," Andrus said.

"But he was—" Hot John said.

Andrus slapped Hot John across the head with his cane.

"Let him go," he said.

Hot John set Bronson down. He walked out of the room, closing the door behind him. Andrus turned back around to the blueprints.

"Don't know where you were but you missed my announcement of our latest conquest," Andrus said, "as well as your big debut. No matter…as long as you make it there for the Fourth of July. Thousands of people elbow-to-elbow in Dixon Park. The police stretched thin. Lots of distractions. Imagine our brothers as they slip through the crowd. Such a perfect fit. I really must send Mayor Lane a thank you note for putting together such a perfect event for us."

"Did you hurt that cowboy guy?" Bronson asked.

Andrus leaned down close to his face. "I'm the one who asked for it to be done, yes. Why? Does that bother you?"

"Why did you do it?" Bronson asked. "Sure, I fought him a couple times but he seemed like a nice guy."

"He let you get away," Andrus said.

"Because of me? You did that… awful thing to him because of me?"

"You are important to the guild's future," Andrus said. "I had to punish him. Imagine how it would have looked to the rest of the guild. They would have thought I was weak, and they would have been right."

"You… you aren't a good guy," Bronson said as he fumbled for the door knob behind his back.

"Maybe not by *their* standards," Andrus said, "but we work for the greater good."

"Anybody who could do that to a person can't be a good guy," Bronson said. "I won't help you anymore."

Andrus turned around. Bronson edged toward the door.

"Why not? By being here with us, Bronson, you've already broken the laws of man. Everybody knows you. You're a bit of a local celebrity. They know you work with us. You show your mask up there and you'll be locked up in juvenile hall for the next five years. Nobody up there wants you."

Andrus might be right, Bronson thought, but he figured he was a lot better off on the street than in the subway tunnels. Bronson slipped his fingers up the back of his shirt. "I know. I'm a little scared, is all," he said, trying to buy himself a few more seconds.

"We don't have the luxury of fear," Andrus said. "We're in this together, and we will win."

Bronson smiled and nodded. "Yes we will," he

said.

Andrus pointed to a small trapezoid on the blueprints. "This is where the band will enter," he said. He pointed to a small area at the back of the stage. "And this is the police cordon."

"Wow, sounds like you've been busy," Bronson said as he pulled the knife out of its sheath. "One thing you didn't think of though."

Andrus chuckled. "My boy, what could I possibly be missing?"

"Where do we stick you?" Bronson asked. He rammed the knife into Andrus's arm then ran to the door. Andrus lunged after him. "Bronson, we could've saved the world together."

"Odds are one of us still might," Bronson said, then he ran down the hall until he was out of sight.

Bronson rushed into the cavern with the subway car. He knew he had to be quick. This was the first place they'd look for him. He threw his wet cloths in his trunk then locked it shut. He pulled the mask over his head, breathing in the sweet smell of plastic and sweat.

Dogboy pulled the trunk over to the entrance of the tunnel so he could grab it on his way out. He turned back to the subway car, jumped in, then ran into the back. Blaze was unconscious. Dogboy pulled out his knife, then cut the ropes and lowered Blaze onto the ground.

He ran over to his trunk and hoisted it up with the handles. It felt lighter every time he moved it. He supposed he might be getting stronger. He looked out into the tunnels. He saw a light coming from the direction of the meeting hall. He'd have to head the other way. He'd never been down there before but desperate times and all that.

He ran around the corner and hid just as Andrus and a few of his men rounded the corner. He pulled out his knife and held it up by his chest, ready to use it if needed, as he listened to them approach.

"All his stuff is down here. I saw it," Hot John said.

Dogboy stayed in the shadows as he peered out to make sure they were gone. He figured he had a few minutes while they searching the area to make his escape from the underground. He ran down the tunnel, lugging his trunk behind him.

When he reached a spot where the tunnel branched out into three separate tunnels He evaluated them, then decided on the darkest tunnel to the left. He disappeared into the shadows as Andrus's men combed the cavern behind him.

Erica waited on Platform A5 for the train that would take her to the hospital for another late-night shift. The attack a few weeks ago made her reluctant to travel around at night, but things had been relatively quiet since then. She'd relaxed back into the old routine. She sat on a bench waiting on the 5:45 to Sully Bend. She never stood next to the platform. Every couple months she'd hear about somebody who fell down on the tracks or was pushed. Gruesome stuff.

About nineteen inches from her head a metal grate flew off the wall. Dogboy jumped out, pulling his trunk behind him.

"You again?" she asked.

Dogboy waved. "Oh, hi. Sorry, can't talk. On the run." He ran to the edge of the platform. Across the tracks there was an escalator that went up to the street level. Dogboy looked down the tunnel. No train as far as he could see. If he timed it just right he could get himself and his trunk over onto the other side before one came through.

Dogboy jumped down onto the tracks then lowered his trunk down behind him. He pulled the trunk across the track with both hands, stopping to lift it up over the big bumps.

A wind whipped down the tunnel when he was halfway across. A train rushed down the track toward the station. He wrapped his arms around the trunk then threw it up on his shoulder. He winced and groaned as he carried it over to the other side. He leaned it on the ledge then pushed it up onto the platform.

The train was about thirty seconds away now. Plenty of time to climb up off the tracks and—

"Dogbrat," Hot John yelled down from the opposite platform, "where ya going, pal?"

Dogboy jumped up the wall then pulled his trunk with him over to the escalators.

Andrus climbed out of the hole in the wall next to Erica, who looked up at the weird hooded figure.

"How many of you guys are there?" she asked.

"Many, my dear child," Andrus said, "only two with masks though."

Hot John climbed up onto the opposite platform as Dogboy reached the escalators. It was narrow, but there was enough room to put his trunk on. Dogboy stepped onto the escalator then turned around. Hot John ran toward him, knocking people out of his way as he approached. Dogboy climbed over his trunk. As he reached the opposite end of the trunk Hot John grabbed his leg.

"You ain't going nowhere, buddy," he said. Dogboy pulled on his leg so hard he thought his knee might pop. He couldn't break Hot John's grip. He began to panic but then realized he still had his secret weapon. He closed his eyes and tried forcing a flash forward to find a way out.

Hot John yelled. Dogboy's eyes snapped open. Hot John stared at smoke that wafted off of his good hand. Free from the John's grasp, Dogboy ran up ahead of his trunk. Hot John leaned against the trunk for support as he sucked his burn. Dogboy shook the trunk and Hot John went tumbling down the escalator.

Hot John landed at the bottom of the escalator hard. He sat up. Andrus stood in front of him.

"You had him, you idiot," Andrus said.

Hot John held out his palm to Andrus. The flesh was black and blistered.

"Kid learned a new trick," he said.

Most of the lights were out in The Old Curiosity Shop. Mr. Horum sat behind the counter counting out the drawer. The bell above the front door sounded. A man stepped into the store. He walked toward the back shelves away from the light.

"No magic left tonight," Mr. Horum said. He put his hand on the baseball bat underneath the counter.

"Do you know a boy named Bronson, sir?" the man asked in a muffled voice.

"Good kid," Mr. Horum said, "bad some days, but good kid. Don't tell Horum he in trouble."

The man... Andrus... stepped into the light.

"You could say that. Don't worry though. My guess is he'll come here to talk with you about resuming his employment soon. When he gets here I have a message I need you to deliver."

Mr. Horum tightened his grip on the bat. "What message?" he asked.

"Tell him his family misses him," the man said. He pointed a pistol at Mr. Horum. Horum pulled out the bat from behind the counter.

He heard a loud noise. A sharp pain... like a bee sting in his chest. He thought it might be his heart but when he reached down to his chest he a warm wet spot. He fell to the floor, blood dripping from his wound. He muttered curse words in his native tongue as the bell above the door rang.

BILL MEEKS

17

The Reunion

Bronson returns to the shop. Bronson returns to the hideout.
Bronson returns to his school. The team plans their attack.

A few hours later the bell above the door rang again. Bronson stepped in.

"Hello?" he said. "Mr. Horum? Door's open. Look, I wasn't trying to be a jerk or nothing before. I—"

A moan rose up from behind the counter. Bronson ran back and jumped over the counter. Mr. Horum was still, wheezing with his hand over his wound. Bronson leaned down and held his hand.

"No," Bronson said, "Wake up. It's me. Bronson."

Mr. Horum took in a big breath and opened his eyes.

"Magician's son," he said, "what you do to Horum now?"

"I swear I didn't have anything to do with this," Bronson said. "I wouldn't. I couldn't."

Mr. Horum pulled himself up onto his elbows. "We ask your friend if you do this. Guy wears mask. Like you."

Andrus. Bronson knew they'd come after him, but it never occurred to him that they would know who his friends were. If they knew Mr. Horum who else did they know?

"How bad?" Bronson asked.

"He buy cheap gun, your friend," he said. Mr. Horum moved his hand and showed Bronson the wound. Deep, but stop at bone I think.

"Come on," Bronson said. "We need to get you someplace safe."

"Your friend come back, you think?"

Bronson smiled at the old man. He led him to the door. "That guy? Maybe. But you're my friend, Mr. Horum. No matter what happens we'll cover each other, right?"

Mr. Horum grunted and let go of Bronson. He took a few steps on his own. Bronson moved back in to help him, but Mr. Horum waved him off.

"Yes, boy-oh," he said. "We cover each other. Where we go?"

"Well, I'm a superhero," Bronson said, "so I say we go to my secret hideout."

"You got hideout?" Mr. Horum asked.

"You call this hideout?" Mr. Horum asked.

Mr. Horum laid in the far corner with his bloody shirt beside him. Bronson sat next to a small fire near the entrance. A small kettle sat on a metal grate above the fire. Bronson tore an old t-shirt into strips that he sterilized in the boiling water before using them to clean Mr. Horum's wound.

"You live here whole time?" Mr. Horum asked. "Right around corner whole time. Crazy pants."

"Not the whole time," Bronson said. He picked up the kettle and knelt down beside Mr. Horum. "Just since my uncle kicked me out. This is going to hurt, okay?"

Bronson took one of the steaming rags and laid it

on the gash in Mr. Horum's chest.

Mr. Horum winced. "You right about that," he said. "You crazy? Where you learn first aid? Internets?"

"The scouts," Bronson said as he cleaned the wound. "This'll keep it from getting infected. Hopefully."

"Heesh. I get no infection if you kill me too, hmmb?" Mr. Horum leaned his head back and closed his eyes. He breathed slow and hard through his nose.

"Bronson," he said, "why you no tell me you need home? I give you place to stay no problem."

Bronson threw the rag into a plastic bag. He grabbed another cloth then applied it to the wound. A small rat ran up and started sniffing the bag. Bronson shooed him away then went back to cleaning the wound.

"Aww, I didn't want to bug you or nothing," he said. "Besides, who would want to leave all this, right?" He put the cloth in the bag. "So what did that man say to you?" he asked.

"He say he need you back," Mr. Horum said. "Said

he will hurt... girl I think?"

"That's what I figured," Bronson said. He put a bandage on the wound.

"You have girlfriend?" Mr. Horum asked. He winked at Bronson. "Hootcha, hootcha."

Bronson stuck his tongue out at him. "She's just a girl I know. From school."

"No questions from me, boy-oh. Except... how you know this guy?"

"He tricked me," Bronson said. "He told me we'd save the world, but I guess that's what most bad guys think... that they are doing the right thing. Maybe I wanted it to be true a little too. Living like this... it's so hard. When somebody offers you a path out of that... I had to give it a shot. He promised me a family. It seemed like he wanted to help, but if I'd known it would come back and bite the people I care about I never would have even thought about it. I never wanted things to be like this."

Bronson knelt down to give Mr. Horum a pillow and a blanket. Mr. Horum reached out for Bronson's hand.

"You be the one to get the bad guy, I betcha."

Bronson crept between the lockers. Considering he'd had some attendance problems the last couple weeks he didn't want to get caught. He didn't imagine he could just play off showing up on the last day before summer break. He turned the corner. Principal Kane stood next to the boy's bathroom looking at a poster on the wall.

Bronson ducked back out of sight. His foot fell back on a snack pack wrapper that crinkled under his foot. Bronson winced as Principal Kane whipped around.

"Mr. Black, fancy seeing you here," Principal Kane said.

"Well, I was heading to class now, sir," Bronson said.

"Do that, but come see me at the end of the day. I think you know we have some business to discuss."

"Yeah. Okay, sir. Sure," Bronson said. As he walked away he couldn't help but think Principal Kane was acting a little strange, but he put it out of his head and went to find Cindy.

Cindy picked up the script for that day's newscast then went around the room and switched on each of the lights. The door opened and Bronson walked in. He checked the hallway one more time then shut and locked the door behind him.

"Sit down," he said. "We need to talk. Now."

"Freak," Cindy said. She hoped this latest distraction would take a hint but he held his ground. She pulled up a chair. "You've got two minutes," she said. "It'd better be *real* important."

"Okay. There's a bad, bad guy who's trying to get to me."

"Who? Bugs?" Cindy asked. "I thought this was going to be something exciting."

"No, not Bugs," Bronson said, "somebody worse, and he knows you know me so he might try to get you too."

Cindy waved her fist at Bronson. "What'd you tell him twerp?" she asked.

"Nothing. Nothing. He just found out I know you. And Horum. But that's it I think. 'People I know in the city' is a pretty short list."

Cindy put down her fist. "Well, why would

somebody be after a nobody like you anyway?"

Bronson thought it might come to this. He bowed his head then looked up in what he hoped was a dramatic fashion. "Because... I'm Dogboy."

Cindy laughed. A lot. She laughed standing up. She fell down to the floor and laughed some more. She got up on her knees still laughing. "You?" she asked. "Dogboy? Ha! Wait'll I tell the ot—"

"No," Bronson said. "Don't tell people. The police think I'm a bad guy now. Do you want to get me arrested or something?"

"Do you really expect me to believe you're being for real?" Cindy asked.

"Yeah," Bronson said. "For really real."

"So, are you a bad guy? They said on the news you've been robbing people."

"I thought I was doing a good thing. This guy who is after me kind of leads a bunch of thieves from underneath the city. He calls them--"

"—the Guild of Thieves," Cindy said. "I knew they were real." She grabbed a notebook from her desk. "How many members would you say this guild has?"

"We don't have time for this," Bronson said. "We

need to go."

"Look, kid," Cindy said, "this is big. There's always time to cover a big story. You came here to rescue me, Dogboy? Don't bother. I can take care of myself."

He took her notebook, then ripped out the page she'd started writing on and ripped it up.

"Hey, that's mine," Cindy said.

Bronson handed the notebook back to her. "Cindy," he said, "I didn't come here to save you. I need your help to bring him down."

Back at Dogboy's secret lair Mr. Horum, Cindy, and Bronson sat around a collection of items Bronson had taken from Mr. Horum's shop as well as a crudely drawn copy of the blueprints Bronson had seen in Andrus's office.

"So," Bronson said, "we all know our jobs?" Bronson picked up a rope and some new throwing knifes and put them in the pouches in his cape. He pulled his mask down over his face.

"Come here, boy-oh," Mr. Horum said. He pulled out a dingy brown handkerchief from his shirt pocket. He unfolded it in the palm of his hand. There was a small silver dollar, which he picked up and handed to Dogboy. "This my lucky coin. Was gift from my Bala's papa. He give it to us when we leave for America. You take it. Maybe it help you out."

"Aw, Mr. Horum," Dogboy said, "I couldn't."

Mr. Horum took Bronson's hand and placed the silver dollar on his palm. He closed Bronson hand and held it with both of his. "You take it. You take it. You may be big time hero guy but still we can help."

Bronson took the silver dollar and put it in his pocket. He walked over to Cindy, who was looking through his trunk. She looked up and eyed his superhero costume.

"That outfit is awful," she said.

Dogboy straightened his cape. "I kind of threw it together," he said.

"So you lived down here?"

"It's not too bad after the first couple of nights. Better than sleeping outside anyway."

"And this whole superhero thing? A little crazy, right? You okay up here?" She tapped her temple.

"My dad left me this stuff. Called it my legacy. He

wants me to do this. I can't let him down."

"Sorry, kid. I didn't mean nothing by it."

"It's fine," Bronson said. "I think about it a lot anyway. You didn't remind me of it or anything."

Cindy took Dogboy's hand. "You came up with a pretty decent plan, kid, but be careful. You need to make it out of there alive if I'm going to get that exclusive interview, right?"

Maybe it was her concern for him, maybe it was because they were about to try to bring down a *lot* of bad guys and he was feeling pretty courageous, but Dogboy thought it might be a good idea to lean in for a kiss. He got about two inches from her face and chickened out. He patted Cindy on the shoulder. "Just joking," he said. "Come on, gang. Let's go."

Dogboy ran over to the entrance and climbed out into the alley.

Mr. Horum walked up beside Cindy. "You know he like you, right?" he asked.

Cindy blushed. "I dunno. Maybe," she said.

Dogboy stuck his head down through the entrance. "Guys, enough standing around. The day isn't going to save itself."

18

The Thrill of the Fourth

Our party arrives at Dixon Park. Osbert gets one over on the police.
Cindy confronts Hot John. Andrus and Dogboy take the stage.

The sun went down in Dixon Park. Thousands of people poured down the walkways, past the food vendors, then out onto the grass. Posters for the annual "Freedom Concert" were pasted up everywhere. There were cops everywhere. They even had men up on horseback looking out over the crowd for any signs of trouble. If they'd concentrated on the ground instead they'd have seen the real danger in the area.

A metal grate behind the food vendors popped open. Ten pudgy fingers wrapped around the sides of the hole. Osbert pulled himself up onto the pavement. He had a leather bag on his shoulder. His outfit was a little more kitschy than his usual attire: jean shorts, a t-shirt with "Stop Looking At My Shirt!" written on it, and a big floppy white hat. He'd wanted to try and stay under the police's radar since they'd be looking for him.

He hid behind a food truck then checked out the crowd. A policeman at ten o'clock. A policewoman at two o'clock. He pulled a small electronic speaker out of the leather bag. He'd designed it for just such an occasion. A small digital timer was strapped to the case of the speaker. Osbert hit the green button on the timer then rolled the device along the ground into the crowd.

The timer counted down from fifteen to one. When it hit zero a siren drowned out the sound of the concert. The nearby police ran to investigate the source of the sound. Osbert slipped out from behind the food truck and made his way down vendors' row.

Mr. Horum pulled up to the delivery gate at the back of the park. A security guard tapped on his window. He rolled it down and smiled.

"Good evening, buddy," he said.

"Name?" the security guard said.

"Horum, but we here with..." Mr. Horum gestured to Cindy, who sat in the passenger's seat.

"WRDB, Cindy McNeil. I'm the intern," Cindy said, waving the camera at the guard. He looked down at the list. He flipped through a few sheets then made a mark with his pencil.

"All good, go in," he said. He went back to his station and flipped a switch.

"You right. Very super easy," Mr. Horum said.

Cindy packed the camera back in its case as the van rolled through the gate.

"Always is when you travel with big shots, Mr. H.," she said.

Dogboy clambered through the scaffolding that hung above the big stage they'd set up for the concert. He was moving pretty fast and didn't want to stop, but according to his watch it was time to check in. He flipped the orange switch on the side of his walkie-talkie.

"Dogboy here," he whispered. "Can you hear me?"

The radio crackled.

"Right, right," Mr. Horum's voice said through the cheap plastic speaker, "we almost there."

Dogboy hit the orange button again. "Cool. I'll see you at the end. Dogboy over and out."

Mr. Horum pulled his van up into the grass next to the crowded fairway. He jumped out of the van and opened the side door then pulled out three metal rings.

His part in the plan was pretty simple: Don't look suspicious and wait for Dogboy to come running. He'd decided to bring some gimmicks so he could do some street magic for the crowd like the old days with his Bala. They'd go down to the wharf on Saturdays and perform card tricks in exchange for money, food, or clothing.

He held out his arms to the people walking. "Come, watch magic trick. Come all, come one," he said, holding the rings up over his head. A small crowd gathered.

He moved the rings back and forth through the air. He tapped them together to show they were solid. A metallic *TING* rang out. He collected all three rings then held them out in front of him and put his hand through the center of them. As he pulled it back out he let go of all but one of the rings, which suddenly had the other two rings attached to it. The crowd around him offered a dull spatter of applause. Mr. Horum didn't care about the cold reception. He bowed to his audience then moved on to the next trick.

Cindy stood above the crowd in the press box, pointing her camera around to get some b-roll of the crowd they could splice in throughout the night if they had to cut away for some reason. As she did she kept her eye out for any guild member but to be honest most of the people in the crowd looked up to no good.

Kathleen ran up to her.

"You're ready, right?" she asked.

"What's that?" Cindy pointed at the center of Kathleen's forehead.

"Oh my God what is it?" Kathleen asked.

"Don't freak" Cindy said, "but there's a huge red blotch on your forehead.

Kathleen dug through her bag.

"Don't freak out?" she said. "Half the freaking country is going to see this thing. You know this might go national, right? Oh, oh—Gotta… sit down." Kathleen lowered herself onto a chair. She counted between breaths. "One… two… three… four… five…"

Cindy put her hand on Kathleen's shoulder. "Don't worry about it. Nobody's going to notice. Forget about it. It's time to go on."

"Already?" asked Kathleen. She dabbed under her eyes with the back of her hand. "Sorry, I don't know why I got so upset. I'll see you out there."

Cindy pulled her walkie talkie out of her pocket. "I'm clear. Ms. Evening News is having a slight panic attack. I might have five minutes before she notices anything but herself. We're good to go."

"I'm on my way to the nest," came Dogboy's voice over of the radio.

Dogboy wasn't sure he was going to make it to "the nest," his second lookout point. Hot John was standing on the other side of the crate he was hiding behind. He decided to hold for a couple of minutes before trying to find another route.

A stagehand rolled a cart down the hallway. Hot John stepped out in front of him then put his foot on the front of the cart to stop it. He reared back his mallet hand then hit the stagehand over the head, sending him to the ground. Hot John pulled the lanyard with an "All Access" badge from around the guy's neck and put it around his. He grabbed the cart's handles, looked around, then pushed it along toward the backstage area.

Now that Hot John was gone Dogboy crawled over to a rope ladder hanging from the wall and started up it.

Axlo and Nuncio walked up to the street from the subway station.

"Yo," Nuncio said, "you got any of that water left?"

"Let me check," Axle said. He knelt down and dug around in his backpack. Nuncio's eyes got wide. He tapped Axle on the shoulder.

"Forget the water," he said. "We got to go. Now."

"Chill," said Axle. "We got plenty of time."

"Yo, look at this."

Axle looked up from his back pack. A group of a few dozen men pushed through the crowd. They all had weapons: clubs, knifes, Blackjacks. They swung them freely through the people as the chanted.

"For Andrus. Arrest this regression for Andrus," they said over and over.

Axle looked at Nuncio. "Bug out," he said. "You know the place."

Axle and Nuncio bolted off in opposite directions as the thieves moved in.

Ned Clark paced in the wings. He took a swig of hot tea and honey from a Styrofoam cup. A stagehand walked up to him.

"One minute, Mr. Clark," the stagehand said.

Ned took a small flask from his jacket. He offered it to the stagehand.

"I'm good, sir," he replied.

"Suit yourself, kid." Ned took a swig from the flask then put it back in his jacket. "They got numbers on this thing yet?" he asked.

"No, but there are about a million or so watching the live feed."

The lights went out. The drummer at the back of the stage started in with a steady rat-a-tat. Ned picked up his microphone, took a sip of his tea, handed the cup to the stagehand, and coughed twice.

The horns kicked in on stage. The curtains opened. The spotlight bled through. Ned ran out and faced the crowd with a wink and a smile.

"Let's get this Independence Day started, Colta City," he yelled into the microphone.

A curtain at the back of the stage fell to reveal two large clay cannons. They pointed at the center of the stage from either side. Two red rockets shot out and passed each other in the air before exploding into little white balls of fire. A blizzard of confetti blew out into the crowd.

The thieves were scattered throughout the audience. They slowly came together like synchronized swimmers, linking arms and trapping small groups of people together.

You could only see this from above, which is why Ned Clark was so distracted. He thought the men might be some acrobatic group or something that they hadn't told him about in rehearsal. These things happen. Ned, a true pro, went over to talk to the band so they could get to their places before he moved on.

Cindy could see them from where she was stationed too. She picked up her radio. "Dogboy. The guild is here. Repeat. The guild is here," she said.

Silence. Cindy considered she'd given away his location, but she hoped he was smart enough to turn the thing off when there were people around.

"Gotcha. Waiting on the big hen. Dogboy over and out," Dogboy said.

Well, she thought, nothing to do but sit here and wait for the real fireworks to start.

She picked up her camera and looked through the viewfinder. There was a man in a floppy white hat moving through the crowd. Cindy thought he looked familiar, but she put it out of her head and tried to find the "big hen." She looked back at him after a moment. He was approaching the police barricade. She *knew* she knew him. She just had to figure out how.

Osbert approached the barricade holding his small leather bag close to his chest. He waved at the policewoman standing in front of the sawhorse barricades. Her badge identified her as Officer Link.

"Pardon me, Officer... Link, is it?" Osbert said.

She put her hand down by her gun. "Can I help you, sir?" she asked.

"I wonder if I might pass through the barricade here. My group is waiting for me on the other side. See?" Osbert pointed across the way. Hot John stood there. He waved at Osbert. Osbert waved back. "One second," he shouted. He turned back to the officer. "That's my brother-in-law over there. God love him but family's family, right?"

The officer looked into Osbert's eyes. She walked over and moved one of the sawhorses out of the way then motioned Osbert through.

"Go along, sir. No stops along the way though. I'll be watching," she said.

Osbert tipped his hat to her as he passed. "My dear lady," he said, "I wouldn't dare."

Back on stage Ned Clark was in full-on presenter mode.

"Now we can't forget the real reason we're all here tonight," he said as he pulled a stack of index cards from his jacket pocket. "Kleinfelder's syndrome is a disease that affects one out of every thousand men—"

Dogboy listened to the impassioned and well-rehearsed speech from the catwalk high above the stage. Now that the curtains were drawn and the set pieces were lowered it was basically a ghost town up there, and that suited Dogboy just fine.

His walkie talkie chirped and he pulled it off his belt.

"Dogboy," he said. "Go ahead."

Cindy's voice came through the walkie talkie. "I figured it out," she said proudly.

"Figured what out?" Dogboy asked.

"There's this guy. It's that dweeby guy that took you. He's here, and they just let him into the police area."

"Osbert," Dogboy said. "What's he doing down there?"

"Walking," she said.

"Well, keep an eye on him. He's not who we need to worry about. Dogboy over and out."

"Wait," she said. "Shouldn't you… you know… catch the bad guy?"

Dogboy counted to ten then hit the button on the radio. "Wait for the hen to fly. Dogboy *over* and *out*."

"Fine, I'll just go catch him myself," she said.

"Cindy. Do not move. I need you right where you are. We discussed this."

No reply.

"Cindy?" he said again.

No reply.

What did she think she was doing? Still, she was right. Dogboy didn't want any of the thieves leaving the park unless it was in a paddy wagon. He decided to flash forward and make sure she'd be okay.

First, he took a handkerchief and held it under

his nose. He laid back on the platform; hoping staying low would keep him from falling off if things got weird again. He focused on his breathing. An orange flash—

It was quicker this time. Ambulances pulled into police area. Everything was on fire. There were a few police vans turned on their side, doors open. There were people—

Dogboy snapped back. He felt fine. No headache. No nosebleed. He felt great actually, but it wasn't the time for celebrating.

The police area in his vision, the one where Osbert and Cindy were both heading, was only a few hundred feet away.

A few minutes later Officer Link stood at her post. Dogboy moved along the tree line until he got past her. He crept up the gravel driveway. Every step made a crunching sound that made his heart jump a little each time.

Something grabbed Dogboy's head from behind. Not just his face or his scalp but his whole head. He felt his feet leave the ground. It was Hot John, who was staring back at Dogboy as he held him in the air.

"Andrus said you might be poking around," Hot John said. "Bet he'll be glad I got you before you could cause any trouble."

"He's not who you have to worry about, bright eyes," said Cindy from behind them. Hot John whipped his head around to look at her. Dogboy decked him. Hot John lost his grip and Dogboy fell to the ground. He grabbed Cindy's hand and they ran away from the dazed dimwit.

"Thanks," Dogboy said.

"What do we do now?" Cindy asked.

"The plan," Dogboy said. "Please get back up there and radio me as soon as you see the big hen."

"You're lucky you're a superhero," Cindy said. "I don't let most people boss me around, especially if I have to save their butts all the time."

"I know," Dogboy said, "you saved my butt. Awesome. Now go!"

They both split up. Cindy headed back toward the press box, while Dogboy went to investigate the parking area a little closer. He leaned down to look under a jeep.

Hot John jumped out from behind the jeep. "Why ain't you quit yet?" Hot John asked. "I've done beat you up twice now."

"I guess I don't know when to lay down," Dogboy said. "It's a problem. Maybe I should—" Flash forward. Hot John brings the mallet down on Dogboy's head, knocking him out. Another flash—

Hot John swung the mallet toward Dogboy hard and fast. He moved his head out of the way as the mallet grazed his shoulder. More than grazed, it seemed. Dogboy looked at his shoulder. He waivered. His knees hit the dirt. Then his chest. Then his head. Hot John leaned over him. The band continued on stage.

Osbert peeked out from behind the police vans. "Do be careful, Jonathan. He is a wily one." He put his pouch on the ground then pushed it under the van with his foot.

"Jonathan, congratulations. We've already won. Move. Quick. And take him with you."

Osbert wandered back down the trail to the barricade. He tipped his hat to Officer Link. "They went around," he said with a shrug. She smiled at him and moved the sawhorse. He wiggled through then made his way through the crowd and as far away from the police area as possible.

Back on stage, Ned Clark bopped his head to the beat as the band played the last few bars of their jazzy rendition of "Grand Old Flag." He ran to the front of the stage and held up his hands. The crowd cheered.

"Give it up for the Colta City Big Blues Band," he said, "and phone lines are open, people. But first, here to cool everybody down on this hot July evening, please welcome the mind-blowing—Colta City's own—Liquid Dynamite!"

"I'm afraid there's been a change in the lineup," said a voice over the P.A. Andrus appeared, shoulders back, cape billowing behind him. He put his arm around a confused Ned Clark.

"Colta City," he said, "tonight we make history."

Sergeant Martin tapped Officer Link on the shoulder.

"Did I see you let a guy come through here?" the

sergeant asked.

"Yeah, Sarge. He was cool. Just some lost guy looking for his family," she replied.

"Link," Martin said, "do you know why we call this a closed area?"

"Why?" she asked.

"Because it darn well needs to stay closed, Link! Do you understand?"

"Sorry, sir," Link said.

"One: You're off duty as of now. Two: On your way out have them send a team of men in here to sweep the area. Three…"

A sound like thunder drowned him out. Cars exploded. People screamed. Fires burned.

Hot John ran through the crowd with Dogboy slung over his shoulder. He breathed in the inky smoke that filled the air around him. Hot John rolled his shoulders and pushed past all the slow pokes.

As he passed a streetlight Dogboy reached out and grabbed it, holding on as tight as he could. He slipped out of Hot John's grip, did a flip in the air, and landed upright a few feet away. Hot John kept going and tumbled into a garbage can head first.

An old man watched from a park bench. Dogboy noticed him and waved.

"Should I move?" the old man asked.

"Don't worry, sir. I think he'll keep," Dogboy said. "But now I need to get back before the bad guy shows up."

The old man lifted his finger and pointed up at the stage. "If that's him then you're too late, son."

Andrus stood in the center of the stage, pushing his foot into Ned Clark's neck.

"Oh crap," Dogboy said.

"Do you have anything else you want to say to your fans?" Andrus asked. He held the microphone up to Ned's face.

"No, sir, you go ahead," Ned said.

Andrus took his foot off Ned's throat then turned out to the crowd.

"My friends... my neighbors... my people... don't panic," he said. "I'm not here to scare you. Trust me. I know everyone here. Even if we've never met or talked I know who you are. You all have fears: the fear of death, the fear of the unknown, the fear of your own failures. You work and study and scrimp and save and look to a day when you won't have to fear anything. Yet we're all still afraid."

Dozens of thieves rushed the security guards in front of the stage. They drew their weapons and used them, capturing the guards and forming a human wall at the front of the stage.

"I offer everyone here and everyone watching at home an opportunity. The promises that the new millennium held are vanishing with astonishing rapidity. We are here to steer the world away from this dark path. We walk amongst you in the city. We are you. If you've ever counted yourself among the downtrodden or the overlooked you belong with us. Don't fear people who are more powerful than you. Join us and fight them. We are the new order. We are the revolution. We are all members of the Guild of Thieves and we are all are needed. Who's with us?"

By now the thieves had broken the entire crowd up into small, controlled groups. A man hugged his wife and newborn baby boy to protect them as everybody pressed in tighter.

"This is our world now," Andrus said. "We exist without nationality, without skin color, without judgment. They may stop one of us, but they can never stop us all. We will win this. Shouldn't you side with the winners? Or do you want to be remembered as traitors?"

Dogboy jumped out from behind the drummer. "Hey, mister," he said, "can I be in your super-secret club?"

"So sorry, folks," Andrus said, "a disgruntled ex-member. This shouldn't take long."

Mr. Horum juggled some crystal balls while he watched Dogboy on the stage. He wanted to help his friend, but he'd promised he'd stay with the van until he got the call. Mr. Horum wasn't a man who went around breaking promises.

Osbert walked by and stopped to the old man juggle.

"You're quite good at that, sir," he said. "Where did you study?"

"I learn on streets. Best school there is," Mr. Horum said.

"That's debatable, but it certainly did the job for you." Osbert reached into his pocket and pulled out a dollar, which he threw in the padded carrying case sitting next to Mr. Horum.

"Have a good night," he said.

"You leave?" Mr. Horum asked. "Good idea, buddy. Things get bad in there, you betcha."

Osbert smiled and tipped his hat to Mr. Horum.

"I assure you, sir. They already have."

Andrus held Dogboy down on the stage.

"You stupid child," he said, "look around you. I have an army. What do you have?" Andrus slapped Dogboy across the face. "You are less than... Loyal, brave, selfless, and dumb... just like a dog."

Dogboy brought his knee up into Andrus's stomach. Andrus flew back onto the ground. He pulled the cap off the end of his cane off and waved the blade in Dogboy's direction.

Dogboy rolled out of the way. He took out a length of trick rope and swung it around his head. Andrus advanced with his cane.

"Oh, a rope. How precious," Andrus said. "Is that

another one of Daddy's little tricks?"

Dogboy bristled at the mention of his father. How did Andrus know about him? Dogboy didn't recall mentioning him, but he could have. Enough. He could get answers later. He threw the rope at Andrus.

The rope hit Andrus square in the jaw then wrapped around his head. It quickly tightened around his mask. He fell to his knees. It squeezed his windpipe shut. He couldn't breathe.

"Pretty neat trick, huh?" Dogboy said. He walked over to Andrus, pushed his foot into Andrus's shoulder, then kicked him over and onto the floor of the stage. The crowd cheered.

Dogboy could get used to this.

19

Andrus Revealed

Making sense of everything. A new trick.
The final battle. Going home.

Cindy pointed her camera at the action happening down on the stage. Her radio squeaked. She took it from her belt then switched it to channel four.

"Axle?" she asked.

"Yeah," Axle said, "we gonna do this or what?"

"There was that big explosion. Now Dogboy's guy is up on stage messing with everybody," Cindy said.

"We should go help him, right?" Axle asked.

"Dogboy looks like he's got a handle on it and he

is getting a little prissy about 'sticking to the plan.' If we're going to bring him over we should probably stay on his good side. I think we might need to postpone."

"Alright, but we can't postpone forever ya' know," Axle said. "Say, is your boy trying to kill that dude?"

Andrus pulled against the rope, but pulling on it made the rope get even tighter. He sunk to the ground as he pushed up on his mask. His face hit the ground and he stopped moving. Dogboy took a step toward him, ready to cut the rope if he needed to.

Andrus twitched and made a gagging sound. He pushed up on the mask again and it fell to the ground. He caught his breath, then lifted his head and smiled at Dogboy.

"Uncle Randolph?" Dogboy asked.

Kathleen walked up behind Cindy.

"I called the explosion in to the station. Wait... is that the Dogboy kid?" she asked.

"Yeah. He just knocked that other guy's mask off," Cindy said.

"Who's the other guy?" Kathleen asked.

"Never seen him. Looks like a creep."

"Well, keep the camera on them. Zoom in as tight as you can. I'm going to call my friends in the Colta City PD to see if they can tell me anything."

Kathleen leaned down and looked in the viewfinder of Cindy's camera. She put her arm on Cindy's shoulder. "This is one of those nights reporters dream of, kid. However this shakes out this is going to be history. Stuff like this just doesn't happen every day. Soak it in."

"I don't understand," Dogboy said. "Why kick me out and then ask me to come live with you in a cave? What kind of mind game is this?"

"Hello, nephew," Randolph said. He picked his mask up off the stage, folded it up, and wiped a bit of blood from the corner of his mouth. "Didn't see this in one of your little visions I take it? Good. I love surprises. Sorry if this is a bit awkward for you. Family spats in public are always dreadful."

"You... why are you doing this?" Dogboy asked.

"I suppose you didn't have your dad's little gift

before the car wreck. Think he saw *that* before it happened? I wonder if he knew I did it? I hope he did."

"What did you do?" Dogboy asked.

"I'll bet you think your parents' deaths were an accident, a mechanical malfunction. But if your father ever taught me anything, Bronson, it's this—"

Randolph kicked Dogboy in the stomach. Dogboy flew back onto his back.

"We make our own luck," Randolph said.

Dogboy closed his eyes and held his hand out towards his uncle. The orange energy licked out and surrounded both him and his uncle.

They shot up like a bolt into the metal pipes above the stage.

Cindy let the camera droop as she took in what she'd just seen. "He never told me he could do *that,*" she thought. Her radio squeaked.

"Yeah?" she said.

Mr. Horum's familiar laugh came over the radio. "Now that an expert trick," he said.

Dogboy lowered them both down on a platform. He shot an orange beam out of his hand that pushed his uncle down on the ground.

"I need to know why," Dogboy said. "Why would you kill them?"

"I was thought your mom and dad had a little more in the way of funding to offer the cause. A mistake. They were poor as church mice. But that mistake created you, right? A little soldier for my army... and with your dad's talents, too. He would have made you waste your gifts just like he wasted his."

"How did he use these powers?" Dogboy asked.

"So you don't even know? That's amazing. He did the same thing you're doing now, kid. That's his old mask. He went around our neighborhood causing trouble dressed just like that. Then brittle little Duncan had one bad experience and stopped it. How can you let powers go to waste like that? The only reason he got them in the first place is because he found the—well, no sense telling you about that."

"You know where these powers came from?" Dogboy asked.

"I do, and they should have been mine. Of course, I got them anyway in the end." Randolph lifted his hand. A darker burst of energy shot out of Randolph's hand. It hit Dogboy in the chest, throwing him back off the platform.

Dogboy fell toward the stage. He closed his eyes and focused his energy, which did a whole lot of nothing. It's difficult to concentrate when you are falling to serious injury or death. He closed his eyes again while imagining a cloud underneath him slowing his fall. When he opened his eyes his orange energy surrounded him, but he wasn't slowing him down much.

Dogboy rolled into it as he hit the stage. He continued rolling straight into one of the giant cannons at the back of the stage. The cannon cracked, throwing some sparks out toward the band. The band ran toward the wings as the bandstand caught fire. The sounds of sirens wailed in the distance.

Dogboy sat up and shook his head. He tasted copper under his mask. A quick check. Warm and wet right under his nose. Ah, well. He'd heal. He crouched down behind the bandstand then crept around the edge of the stage toward the giant bald eagle statue.

Randolph drifted down to the stage surrounded by his dark aura. He picked up the microphone.

"So sorry for the interruption," he said. "Now, where was I? Oh, yes. Winners or traitors? I say time's up. Traitors the lot of them. Commence. Begin. Commence."

More thieves ran through the crowd to join their brothers. They all carried zip ties and started binding the wrists of people in the crowd.

"I planned out this whole big night for you and not one of you wants to join me? Who will stand with us?"

Silence. But then the crowd started clapping. Then they cheered. Randolph smiled and waved to the crowd. "My guild, now we can—"

Dogboy landed between Randolph's shoulder blades leading with his feet. Andrus fell down. Dogboy's entire body glowed bright orange. Randolph clawed at the knife on Dogboy's ankle, but as soon as his hand touched it his skin began to pop and sizzle.

He screamed then pulled his hand to his chest.

"Where'd you learn that trick, nephew? Not even your dad could manage that." Randolph chuckled. "I'm sorry for this, but if you won't play nice you're going to have to play dead."

Randolph shot a burst of energy into Dogboy's back. He pulled out a revolver from his coat then cocked the hammer. Dogboy's aura flowed out and formed an orange bubble around him. He floated closer to Randolph. Randolph kept the gun trained on his nephew. Dogboy's head shook. Tendrils of fire blew out from the eye holes in his mask.

"Tell your daddy I said 'hi,' kid," Randolph said. He pulled the trigger. As the shot rang out the orange ball around Dogboy expanded. It hit the bullet, which melted in mid-air, the metal dripping on the stage. Then the energy slammed into Randolph, sending him flying against the wall. The energy grew larger than the stage as it pulsed out into the crowd. Most of the crowd was unaffected, but the guild members fell to the ground spitting and seizing.

The microphone floated up to Dogboy. He

snatched it from the air. "If you're with Andrus and you're still standing I'm giving you ten seconds." The orange ball contracted. Dogboy floated down and landed gently on the stage.

He laid the microphone down then walked over to his uncle. He pulled the knife from his ankle then pressed it against Andrus's throat.

"Where did you get the power?" he asked. "No lies, or I use this. For the record I'm okay if you lie."

Randolph chuckled. "No lies, but no truth either. Not yet." Randolph's eyes rolled into the back of his head as he drifted off. Dogboy put the knife back in its sheath.

"Some revolution, Uncle Randolph," Dogboy said. He picked up the microphone. The crowd began chanting his name: *Dogboy. Dogboy. Dogboy.*

"Folks—Colta City—Thank you. I don't know everything you've heard about me but I hope you guys know I'm not with those thieves. I was a little confused for awhile but I'm better now. Don't worry. I'm a good guy, or at least I'll try to be a good guy."

Dogboy floated into the air. "Thanks for letting me save you, and remember— I'm Dogboy." He dropped the microphone, flashed a thumbs up at the crowd, then floated up and out over Dixon Park.

He saw the thankful citizens, injured policemen, retreating thieves, and others slipping by below him, then he disappeared into the trees on the south end of Dixon Park.

Cindy put her camera in its case and closed the lid. She walked over to Kathleen, who was typing her notes to send to the station.

"Kathleen," Cindy said, "this was an amazing night. An amazing, dangerous, exciting night."

Kathleen closed her laptop. "Yes, it was. What's with the radio though? That isn't from the station, is it?"

Cindy put her hand over the radio attached to her belt. She hadn't thought anybody would notice.

"There's this boy at school. He wanted to talk while I was working. He's kind of a dork like that. Don't tell on me, okay?"

Kathleen smiled. "I remember what that felt like."

"What?" Cindy asked.

"My first crush."

"Eww, no. He's just a friend."

"Sure he is," Kathleen said. She walked over to the news van and put the laptop inside. "You need a lift?" she asked Cindy.

"Nah, that's okay. I have a ride."

"Who?"

Cindy looked away from Kathleen. "That boy from school. Well, we're both getting a ride from the same person anyway. He's not old enough to drive. Not that I'd ride with him if he did. Well maybe."

"I thought so," Kathleen said. She climbed up into the news van and it rolled away.

Cindy and Mr. Horum sat in Mr. Horum's van waiting on Bronson.

"How long do you think it'll take him?" Cindy asked.

"He come when he come," Mr. Horum replied. Mr. Horum offered Cindy half of a Peppermint Pattie, which she accepted. They sat there chewing on their candy.

A loud THUMP came from the top of the van. A

moment later Dogboy jumped in through the back doors then slammed them shut. Mr. Horum turned on the engine and drove.

"Bronson," Cindy asked, "why didn't you tell me you could fly? That was awesome. And your energy blasts... WHAM! But how was that guy able to do them too? Does this have something to do with Mayor Lane's—"

"It was my uncle," Bronson said. He looked up at her. "He... he killed my parents. Cindy, I'm... a little tired right now. Could we talk about this later?"

Cindy felt awful. "Yeah. Whenever you want. Sorry."

Bronson smiled at Cindy. "No, you're right. It's pretty cool."

"C'mere. After all that you deserve a hug at least." Cindy unbuckled her belt and climbed back next to Bronson. She hugged him. He hugged her back. It was sweet.

Cindy pulled back. She smiled at him then kissed him. He tasted a slight hint of mint. It opened up his lungs, like vapor rub on your chest when you have a cold. He leaned into the kiss as he mirrored the movements she was making with her mouth.

She pulled her head back and took Bronson's hand. "You did good tonight," she said.

Bronson laughed. "You too. You stuck to the plan. Mostly."

Cindy punched Bronson in the arm then climbed back up into the front seat. Mr. Horum looked over at her and winked. She winked back. Mr. Horum got on the interstate, the quickest route to the other side of town. He adjusted the rearview mirror so he could see Bronson.

"Where you live now?" he asked.

Bronson yawned and curled up against the window. "In the hideout, I guess," he said as he closed his eyes.

"When I see you fight I think 'Predsha, why big hero like this live like rat when you have four walls to use?' I have much room. You live with me. Now we family, hmmb?"

Bronson snored from the back seat. Mr. Horum smiled and readjusted his mirror. "We fix it up soon, I betcha."

20

The Press Conference

Mayor Lane holds a press conference. Somebody interrupts it.
Dogboy heads off on a new adventure. Cindy surprises Mr.
Horum.

A week later Mr. Horum, Cindy, and Bronson stood
around the TV at The Old Curiosity Shop watching
Mayor Lane's press conference on WRDB. This was
his fifth press conference since the 4th of July
incident.

"We honor the passing of the three Colta City
residents who lost their lives during the events of the
July 4th incident. The city stands by the families of

these victims in their time of grief. We have the man responsible in custody. Andrus, as he called himself, is still in critical condition at Colta City General. Rest assured that we are making every effort to discover his true identity. When and if he recovers we will prosecute him to the fullest extent of the law. You will know his name."

Bronson practiced juggling three crystal balls Mr. Horum had loaned him. "Let him stay in that coma as far as I'm concerned," he said.

Cindy scrunched up her nose. "What a jerk," she said.

"My uncle?" Bronson asked. "Yeah." Bronson dropped one of the crystal balls. It rolled under a shelf. He kneeled down to retrieve it.

"No, the mayor. First off he poisons a bunch of kids, gets off because they don't have enough 'evidence,' he lets a bunch of slime balls who live down in the sewers or something—no offense—take over the park, and he still gets to stand in front of TV camera with a huge smile on his face. It isn't fair."

"I'm sure Mayor Lane's not such a bad guy," Bronson said.

A small crowd gathered in front of City Hall to watch Mayor Lane give his press conference.

"...while we all appreciate this Dogboy's help, I must condemn his actions. Vigilanteism isn't the answer to threats this criminal or his cult. We all owe a debt to the skilled Colta City Police Department. That's who is really protecting the city. You can trust them. They answer to *me*."

The crowd applauded. Mayor Lane waved. A large hovercraft descended from the sky. It came to a stop behind the mayor. The crew, a group of five teenagers in makeshift costumes, steadied themselves as the ship lowered to the stage. A tall boy with a silver streak through his hair walked to the edge of the hovercraft.

"Did you think we'd forget, you?" he said.

"Who are you? What is the meaning of this?" Mayor Lane snapped. Some policemen ran toward the stage. He just had to keep the kid talking for a minute.

"Name's Coaxle, and we're here for you, your honor." The boy motioned to a girl toward the back with short blond hair and a leather jacket. "Material Girl, the mayor here could use a makeover."

The girl took off her stonewashed jacket. She closed her eyes. The jacket glowed then morphed into a giant fishing net with some weights attached. Material Girl handed the net to Coaxle.

Coaxle swung the net around his head a few time then let it fly. It hit Mayor Lane, who fell back against the podium. The weights tangled themselves around his body.

Coaxle jumped down and tied up the trapped politician. The policemen ran at the stage. Coaxle touched his temples. Electricity, or something like it, arched out from both sides of his head and hit the policemen surrounding him. They cried out then fell to the ground. Coaxle loaded Mayor Lane into the hovercraft. "We'll take care of this villain, folks. You can thank the—"

The roar of the hovercraft's engines drowned him out as it soared into the air then disappeared behind the roof of City Hall.

"I know one of them," Bronson said. "The electric

guy. He taught me some stuff. But you can't just kidnap the mayor."

Bronson stepped into the back. He tossed Cindy a walkie talkie.

"You sure?" asked Cindy. "Maybe you should just let them go."

"I'm going to try to help them fix this," Bronson said. "If Axle isn't careful he's going to get all of them caught."

Mr. Horum took a bag from under the counter and threw it back to Bronson, who took his mask out of it then slid the mask over his head.

Dogboy tied on his cape and checked his pockets. "Fresh box of Glimmers, Mr. Horum." Mr. Horum pulled a crate off the shelf and tossed Dogboy a couple boxes.

"You no die, ok?" Mr. Horum said.

"You got it, Mr. Horum," Dogboy said. He walked out the back door. A few seconds later Cindy ran out behind him, turned him around, lifted his mask, and gave him a kiss.

"How do you know these guys will even want your help?" Cindy asked.

"I don't," Dogboy said, "but if they don't I'll do what I have to."

Dogboy pulled up a street grate near the back of the shop.

"Wait," Cindy said.

"What?" Dogboy asked.

She held up her walkie talkie. "Keep it on Channel 3," she said.

Dogboy waved then jumped down into the darkness. Cindy looked down into the tunnel. Dogboy wasn't there, but a dull orange glow reflected off the water. Cindy watched it fade away to nothing.

She changed her walkie talkie to Channel 7.

"He's coming," Cindy said into the radio, "and you can't let him know. Whatever happens don't let Dogboy find out."

"Done," a voice responded.

Cindy switched the walkie talkie back to Channel 3.

"What Bronson can't know?" said Mr. Horum. He stood in the doorway behind her.

"Don't worry, Mr. Horum. It wasn't anything to worry about. In his best interest for sure." She reached out and touched his shoulder. "Did you say something about Bronson?"

"No, no. I ask you to come inside." Mr. Horum headed back toward the door. "You have hearing problems?"

"Sorry, don't know what's going on with me lately. Forget I said anything," she replied.

ABOUT THE AUTHOR

Bill Meeks is a video producer, writer, podcaster, and all around creator of stuff. He lives with his family in the suburbs of Atlanta, Georgia. His video work has been seen in international cinemas, on domestic television, and across the wider Internet. He considers himself to be the world's biggest authority on Superman, but admits that he's probably more like the 900th.

Twitter: @billmeeks
Website: http://www.meeksmixedmedia.com
Google: http://google.com/+BillMeeks

Get all the latest news from the world of Dogboy at

DOGBOYADVENTURES.COM

or follow us on Twitter:

@DogboyBooks

Printed in Great Britain
by Amazon

13149675R00180